IN THE BARN

AND OTHER STORIES

BY RICH TAYLOR

Sharon Mountain Press

For information: Sharon Mountain Press, Inc., 1 Jewett Hill Road, Sharon, CT 06069.

Library of Congress Catalog Card Number:
92-061634

ISBN 0-9633994-1-1

Publisher's Note: This is a work of fiction. The characters, incidents, and dialogues are products of the author's imagination and are not to be construed as real. Where the names of actual persons, living or dead, are used, the situations, incidents, and dialogues concerning those persons are entirely fictional and are not intended to depict any actual events or change the entirely fictional nature of the work.

Manufactured in the United States of America

Book and Cover Design by Jean Constantine

Contents

The Ferrari in the Barn

The first time I saw Peter was a warm, sunny afternoon in September of my junior year. I was daydreaming my way up Waterman Street in Providence, heading toward a date with Jean at the sculpture studio, when the most incredible *shriek* lit off behind me. My first thought was that SDS antiwar protesters had fire-bombed the John Hay Library again.

I sort of simultaneously ducked and turned, just as the most brilliant red Ferrari went past me with all the impact of a helicopter air strike...unbearable noise, flashing colors, disorienting speed... and then it was gone as suddenly as it had come, skipping the edge of a changing yellow light and arcing onto Thayer Street in a ragged two-wheel drift.

I concentrated like hell to hold my vivid mental image of that red blur sliding around the corner until I got home that night. I dug through my stack of dog-eared *Sports Cars Illustrated* until I found the picture. I was *right*. There was Phil Hill winning the Sebring 12-Hour in a Ferrari Testa Rossa. It had to be *the same car*. Or at least, identical. A bloody red car, splashing past the pits in a pissing rainstorm, Hill casually waving to his crew. I was so consumed with envy I could spit.

The Ferrari owner's notoriety grew rapidly. Within days, it was common knowledge that a kid named Peter Terry had been thrown out of the University of Connecticut and through some quirk of family, fate or finances, accepted at Brown. He had arrived in Providence with a live-in girlfriend who was a part-time fashion model in New York, a Japanese houseboy/chauffeur, his grandfather's 8-liter Bentley limousine for the chauffeur and a Shelby GT-350 for the girlfriend. And of course, the only Testa Rossa north of Luigi Chinetti's Greenwich race shop. So what if it was a few years old? Nobody had ever seen anything like it.

Instead of a dorm room or a cramped off-campus apartment, Peter rented an entire house in the fanciest Old Money neighborhood on Benefit Street. Before long, word had reached even the most out-of-it geek that the wildest parties in Rhode Island, hell, maybe in New England, took place Friday night through Sunday afternoon at Peter's.

Peter's parties were all-night, all-weekend mob scenes of students, sports car nuts, fashion models and the inevitable college-town hangers-on, livened up with local Mafia types in dark suits and white ties who always seemed to leave before midnight with one of the miniskirted models clinging to each arm.

Later on in the evening, couples would discretely or indiscretely disappear upstairs. In the flat gray light of the morning after, they'd silently help themselves to a breakfast buffet laid out by the ever-present chauffeur, then collapse white-faced into various postures of picturesque disarray, sipping Bloody Marys or the chauffeur's secret hangover remedy which depended heavily on horseradish, raw eggs and gin.

I drifted through half-a-dozen parties at Peter's that fall. One didn't need an invitation. A friend of a friend would know someone who was going, and you'd all just meet there in the swirling mob. Day or night, Peter would be standing in the center of the maelstrom, jacketless, his starched dress shirt wet with sweat and spilled drinks, his shirttail hanging out, his blonde hair glued to his glistening forehead, his face the color of quarry tiles. As I remember him, he was always laughing.

His girlfriend, who ironed her hair like Mary Travers, wore the shortest miniskirts imaginable and spent her evenings dancing slowly with dark complexioned, muscular guys named Tony or Mike. She had the most curious eyes, a blue so light it was translucent as an aquamarine. She called herself Marielle, which sounded somehow French, but when she spoke, it was with the broad American accent of the Upper Midwest. I always imagined that she had been christened something like Marie L. Schermerhorn. Marie Louise, maybe.

Weekends went on like this for about three months, with the neighbors writing increasingly irate letters to the *Providence Journal* and the school authorities trying to figure out the extent of *in loco parentis*. Party-goers from as far away as Yale and Columbia were stopping by, and a car-load of coeds from Skidmore moved into the upstairs bedrooms for two weeks.

In a way, it was my fault that it all ended as quickly as it began. About midnight on a crisp Saturday in November, the chauffeur ran out of liquor behind the bar, due to an unusual demand brought on by impending mid-term exams. Peter was nowhere to be found. The chauffeur finally wrote out his account number at the liquor wholesaler and nonchalantly handed me the keys to Peter's Testa Rossa.

I couldn't believe my luck. I elbowed my way down the side steps, hopped into the Ferrari before somebody noticed me and after figuring out the controls, started it up to back out of the driveway. The *blaaatt...BLAAATT* of the exhaust caused an older man walking his West Highland Terrier across the street to turn towards the house. How he could hear that open exhaust above the sound of Mick Jagger screaming *Satisfaction* on Peter's stereo, I'll never know.

As we later learned from the newspaper accounts of Peter's dismissal, not only was this shadowy neighbor a "prominent local attorney," but a member of the college Board of Trustees. When I flicked on the Testa Rossa's headlights, he was an open-mouthed audience for an illuminated tableau in which Peter, a garden bench and a mostly-naked African Studies major from Wheaton figured prominently.

I didn't see Peter again for twenty years. I knew he'd gotten into endurance racing, because his name would appear in the results from LeMans, or the Daytona 24-Hours or Sebring. He was never in the front rank, and I had no doubt that he was buying rides. They were always rides in first-class cars, with name drivers. But somehow, they never seemed to finish out front, and next race, Peter's name would appear as part of another team.

Then two years ago, Jean and I moved to a sprawling old farmhouse in upstate New York, picked mostly for its three big garages and proximity to Watkins Glen. About a month after we moved in, I went over to run my Mazda in a Regional. I was standing in the paddock, talking to the scrutineers, when the air filled with the sound of...*I know that sound.*

Twenty years dropped away. Sliding to a stop beside me was Phil Hill's Testa Rossa, with Peter and Marielle smiling and waving. Peter was heavier, and his complexion was redder, but his open-mouthed laugh was the same. Except for the wrinkles around those translucent eyes when she smiled, Marielle was just as I remembered her...flawlessly pretty as an Irving Penn picture in *Vogue*, and just as remote.

The old Ferrari looked absolutely ravishing, *better* than it had ever been in our college days. It made my teeth ache to look at it...right-hand steering, headrest, cut-down plexiglass windshield and hood scoop, a fender shape so sensuous and flowing it brought tears to your eyes. And the paint really *was* the color of fresh blood.

It was all too much for me...a forgotten snapshot suddenly come to life. I was thrust back into the shell of insecurity I suffered as a poor college kid, pretending a sophistication I neither knew nor understood. I went off to race, blew my start and got beaten by half-a-dozen cars I would have put on the trailer any other weekend. My mind was two decades in the past, staring after a Ferrari Testa Rossa that might just as well have landed from Mars as Maranello.

After that, we saw Peter and Marielle quite a lot. And gradually, we learned that all was not what it appeared at first glance. They hadn't come through those decades without a scar...they were mostly scar tissue. Part of the reason they were friendly to us was that their lives were in such disarray, and they had alienated so many relatives and friends, that there were few people still talking to them. Jean and I possessed the blessed virtue of accepting them as a couple, because twenty years ago, that was the way we'd known them.

After the debacle in Providence, Marielle had gone home to her family in Minneapolis, met a medical student, gotten married and produced three children. The oldest girl was already in college. Peter had finally gotten a degree from one of those small colleges outside Boston, finishing schools for boys too young to manage their own trust funds. His only excitement seems to have been 170 mph top speed runs with the Testa Rossa on Route 128, in the middle of the night. Then he had gone home to live with his mother—a bedridden invalid—not ten miles from Watkins Glen.

He had never married, indeed, he had become pretty much a recluse...I suppose it was penance of a sort. He occupied his days puttering with a growing collection of old Ferraris. It was only a quirk of fate that had brought Marielle's husband the doctor to Elmira hospital, a hospital to which Peter's long-dead grandfather had left millions.

The Ferrari in the Barn

Peter and Marielle met again at a hospital ball, and it was as if the twenty years had never passed. Marielle's husband took the children, moved out and called his lawyer, and all his friends—who used to be *their* friends—stopped talking to her. Peter's family ignored her, too, though his invalid mother hated Marielle with a cold jealousy that was frightening to see if you knew how to look.

Peter couldn't see it. He and Marielle were already planning the new house they were going to build on his family farm. They had set a date for the wedding, six months in the future, and they acted like a couple of love-crazed kids, not middle-age adults who are supposed to know better. There wasn't much room left for anyone else.

The road to Peter's farm wound up, down and around a mountain...most of which he owned. The nearest neighbor was miles away. There was a set of wrought-iron gates, then a driveway that went for a quarter-mile through the woods. The main house, his grandfather's house, had burned years before. Peter and his mother lived in a former guest cottage, mostly constructed of fieldstone and exposed timber. There were uncounted cats, two huge St. Bernards and enough antiques to keep a Park Avenue shop in business for a lifetime.

Behind the house were barns. Big barns. Peter shyly led me on a tour, one rainy afternoon. The barns were cut into the side of the mountain, so typically the top floor might be accessible from one side, the bottom floor from the front. There was a separate shop building, with three bays, a lift and a full set of machine tools.

On the lift was a Ferrari 330GTC, into which

Peter was preparing to insert a V-12 engine he'd just rebuilt. It was going to be Marielle's wedding present. Next to it was another GTC waiting for a new interior. In the barns there were 308GTs, Dinos, three or four 365GT 2+2s, a 365 Daytona NART racer still covered with grime from a long-forgotten Watkins Glen 6-Hour, a roomful of 330GTs, another room with nothing but 250GTs and 410 Superamericas from the late Fifties.

One small landing held a matched pair of Short Wheelbase Berlinettas, immaculately restored in Rob Walker's dark blue and white Scots color scheme, an ASA Mille and enough 365GTB/4 Daytona racing parts to do a full season. Lined up in a barn basement were an early 166 Barchetta, his grandfather's Bentley limousine, the Testa Rossa and Peter's street transportation, a 400GT automatic into which he'd dropped a 454 Chevy V-8.

We saw Peter and Marielle periodically throughout that summer and fall. Each time they'd be driving a different Ferrari, each time they'd maintain a brittle, teasing manner that effectively shut out everybody else. They came to our New Year's Eve party. Talk about *deja vue*. Marielle danced slowly with the neighbors' husbands—they practically waited in queue; Peter installed himself on the living room couch where he could dominate the conversation as his face turned redder and his laugh grew louder.

When they finally left early in the morning of New Year's Day, I walked them out to the car. Marielle hugged and kissed me goodnight with unexpected warmth. Peter laughed. Then he turned and pissed on the wheel of his Ferrari before roaring off into the night, the incongruous boom of the big block V-8 echoing off my barns and down the valley to the lake.

Peter spent that winter building a Corvette for the Sebring 12-Hours, a car that belonged to a friend of his who thought he was a racing driver. They retired early with what Peter dismissed as "terminal driver error." He already had two new projects going. One was a body kit based on the F40 that he wanted to build and sell for used 308GTs. The other was the restoration of an old John Deere tractor that had been sitting in the barn for years. Peter was putting the leftover 4.8-liter V-12 from his 400GT into the John Deere, just for kicks. "Maybe I'll paint 'Lamborghini' on the nose," he said. And laughed.

Marielle phoned me in tears one evening in mid-April. An emergency room doctor who knew them both had called her. The best the police could figure out, Peter had finished his V-12 tractor and taken it up the side of the hill behind the barn to try it. He died instantly when the tractor rolled over and broke his neck, but he had lain there for hours in the mud until his mother, alone in the house, had crawled to the phone and called the police.

After the accident, the wrought iron gates were locked, the body cremated and a nurse hired to look after Peter's mother. There was no funeral. The hurried, almost furtive way it was handled left everyone feeling faintly uneasy, a bad bit of unfinished business like an opera missing the last aria. There was suspicious talk in town, but that soon died out. It was just that we never got to say goodby.

Marielle asked for nothing, except to be allowed to buy the 330GTC Peter had built especially for her. His mother wouldn't even return her phone calls. I called to ask on her behalf, and Peter's mother stopped talking to me, as well. There was a rumor that a Ferrari collector had offered her $15-million for the Testa Rossa and she had turned him down. No one was allowed into the property, let alone into Peter's barns.

I saw Marielle frequently at Watkins Glen last summer. We would sit on her blanket on the hill behind the pits and talk about Peter, and about her divorce, and about people we knew in racing, and about what she was going to do in the future. It was the conversation of two casual acquaintances united only by that briefest of ties, friendship with a dead man.

Yesterday, Marielle called me for the first time in months. She was going to be in the neighborhood, and did I have time for lunch. We met at a little roadside restaurant on the lake. The day was mild; we sat on the deck and ate our salads. Marielle was warmer and less remote than I ever remember her. This was what she must have been like between Peter, when she was a happily-married midwest doctor's wife.

She talked about new friends, about skiing in Colorado, about scuba diving in St. Thomas. She had cut her hair; she was overdressed for upstate New York. A fashion photographer she'd known in the old days had done her portfolio and she had signed with a model agency in Manhattan.

"Good-looking middle-age women are in demand right now," I said.

In the old days, she would have ignored me. Last year she would have laughed at my lack of tact, told Peter, and the two of them would have teased me for weeks.

This time she gave me an appraising stare from the aquamarine eyes. "That's why I like you so much. You're safe."

The sun was already low on the lake when the waitress smiled us out. We walked awkwardly arm-in-arm, and kissed goodby in the parking lot. I put her into her Mercedes and kissed her again. We agreed to meet next week at a different restaurant, further from home.

"If we're not careful," she said, "people will start to talk."

Driving home, I went the long way over the mountain. I'm sure I planned it, but I was still surprised when I reached the end of Peter's driveway. The gates were locked. I parked my old Stingray coupe, climbed the wall and walked up to the barn that was hidden from the house. I swung back the old-fashioned door and went inside.

Peter's Testa Rossa was right where he had always parked it, facing out, ready to go. There was a light coating of dust on everything, but not as bad as I expected. I stepped over the thigh-high door, and slid down under the mahogany Nardi wheel. I pulled the gated shifter into neutral, turned the master switch, and the electric fuel pumps clicked into life. I pushed the big starter button on the dash. The engine turned over for a few seconds, then stopped as the nearly-dead battery lost its charge.

I sat there in the Ferrari until it got so dark I could no longer see the five deer—three females, a nervous young buck and a fawn—grazing in the uncut alfalfa field in front of Peter's barn.

Fat Mutchie and the Morgan

I gotta tell ya about Fat Mutchie. It should be a lesson. Fat Mutchie lives in Brooklyn. Well, Brooklyn Heights, anyway, which is cute, like maybe Russian Hill in San Francisco, but with more dirt. Brooklyn Heights is not a cheap neighborhood; a decent three-story row house might cost you a million-six, a million-seven. Unfurnished. And a row house in Brooklyn is only 15 feet wide.

Fat Mutchie has this brownstone off Atlantic Avenue, you can go up on the roof and you can see the Statue of Liberty on a day when the smog isn't clogging the harbor. Inside, his girlfriend Teresa had a crew of Lebanese carpenters cut right through the floors and make one tall space with balconies like a Hyatt Hotel.

Fat Mutchie is telling me about his house. "This house has everything," he says. "It has a fireplace, it has a whirlpool, it has a sauna, it has a kitchen with an espresso machine that looks like one in the Hard Rock Cafe. It has a waterbed it should leak the whole block would be flooded. It has projection TV in the entertainment center and color TV in the bathrooms. It has a home office so fancy I feel like maybe Donald Trump. You know what this house ain't got? It ain't got no garage."

Fat Mutchie is a car collector. Being a car collector in New York City is worse than being a drug dealer. You go around in secret, constantly looking over your shoulder, making deals in neighborhoods that nice people don't visit. You pay protection money to sleazeballs who work in parking garages. At dinner parties, nice people who walk to work back away when you mention the word "automobile."

Despite these adversities, Fat Mutchie collects Morgans. Twenty years ago, when Mutchie was a teenager, he was almost run over by a Morgan Plus-4 roaring down Eastern Parkway on its way, ultimately, to Bridgehampton Raceway. Mutchie picked himself up and like Scarlett O'Hara in *Gone With The Wind*, shook his fist in the direction of the departing Morgan. "As God is my witness," recited Mutchie, "I'll own one of those fuckers someday."

And so he does. The way it works, Mutchie reads the real estate ads, not the auto ads, in *The New York Times*. He's shopping for a garage. When he finds a parking space advertised for less than $100 a month, he zips over there in Teresa's Mercedes, pays the guy two years rent in advance, plus a little something extra to look out for his interests. Then Mutchie goes shopping for another Morgan. In New York City, it's easier to find an old Morgan than a place to park it.

Fat Mutchie's 1935 Super Sports Morgan/JAP

three-wheeler lives in solitary splendor in a converted chicken coop behind a Chinese restaurant in Sheepshead Bay. His 1959 Plus-4 is hidden in the back of a repair shop in Massapequa, sealed in a giant plastic bag along with a year's supply of Damp-Away.

His 1972 Plus-8 is in the showroom of an exotic car dealer in Sea Cliff. Theoretically, the Plus-8 is for sale on consignment, but Mutchie has set the price so high, not even a Japanese pachinko tycoon would buy a Morgan for this much. Fat Mutchie pays the dealer $100 a month as an advance against a commission that will never come.

The jewel of Mutchie's collection, his 1964 Sprinzel Lawrence Racing Morgan coupe, is in a secret hiding place behind a boat yard up on City Island in the Bronx. It's been there so long, Fat Mutchie would have a hard time remembering what it looks like, he didn't have a picture on his wall. He has a map in his desk drawer in case he forgets how to get there.

All of this drives wild Mutchie's girlfriend Teresa. "Teresa does not worship at the altar of internal combustion," explains Fat Mutchie, shrugging his shoulders. Teresa is a tall, thin, thirtyish, washed-out blonde who used to be Mutchie's secretary when he owned the wholesale fish market on Queens Boulevard. Teresa lived with her mother in a row house in Kew Gardens.

When the mother finally died, Teresa sold the house and moved in with Fat Mutchie. First she remodelled his house. Then she remodelled Fat Mutchie until he doesn't even have to shop at Big & Tall anymore. Then she got him to sell the fish market and invest his millions in tax-free bonds.

For about a year, Fat Mutchie and Teresa lived like they had retired to LeisureWorld. Teresa broke first. Hanging around the house all day listening to Fat Mutchie whine about how things were more fun when he got up at 3 am and spent all day in a freezing cold building that smelled of fish finally got to her.

Maybe six months ago, Teresa enrolled at the New School for Social Research, as a student of Environmental Studies. Soon she was offered a position as secretary to Professor Mason, the tall, balding department head with an earnest manner and well-known weakness for thin blondes.

Within a few months, Teresa is working all day, then going to college in the evening and getting home about 10 at night. Her environmentally-fueled intolerance of internal combustion engines grows along with the shadows under her eyes. She has even started to bitch because she has to be "the little worker troll," while Mutchie stays home all day.

Meanwhile, Fat Mutchie is sitting home in Brooklyn in his office that looks like Donald Trump's, and he is, as they say, "attending to his business affairs." He has bought some apartment houses in Brooklyn so he can go argue with the tenants. He has bought a little house out in Eaton's Neck on the beach, it should maybe someday be a place to retire.

He buys and sells a few stocks, he reads books of investment advice written by guys Mutchie could buy and sell by the dozen, packed in crates like halibut. He goes to investment counseling seminars. He studies everything he can find about Morgans. And he reads *The New York Times* Classifieds, real estate and antique autos only.

One warm Sunday morning in May, Fat Mutchie is drinking capuccino from his fancy espresso machine and reading the antique auto ads. One burns off the page at him: *1953 flat-radiator, twin-spare Morgan racing car. Extremely rare, total restoration. Must sell. $10,000 or best offer.* There is a phone number on Long Island.

Mutchie looks furtively over his shoulder as he dials the phone. Teresa has given him strict instructions not to buy "any more stupid little cars you never drive." Ah. But Teresa is attending mass at St. Bartolph's with Mrs. McCarthy from down the block. Mutchie is safe for at least another half-hour.

The woman who answers Mutchie's phone call has one of those breathless, thrilling voices. Scott Fitzgerald gave Daisy Buchanan a voice like this. "The kind of voice the ear follows up and down," Fitzgerald wrote, "as if each speech is an arrangement of notes that will never be played again. There was an excitement in her voice that men who had cared for her found difficult to forget; a singing compulsion, a promise that she had done gay, exciting things just a while since and that there were gay, exciting things hovering in the next hour."

Fat Mutchie doesn't know from F. Scott Fitzgerald. When he is telling me this story, he says, "This damned woman talks like she's naked in the bedroom, you know what I'm saying?"

The lady with the bedroom voice tells Mutchie that her ex-husband was a car collector. This guy, he gave the Morgan to her because her name is Morgan. "This is so warped, it makes me sick to my stomach," says Fat Mutchie. But not so sick that he doesn't want to see the car she is selling for $10,000.

Breathless Morgan tells him she ended up with the car when the divorce came. Now she needs to buy a real car, something a little more practical than a forty-year-old racing machine. They make a date to meet the next afternoon. The address is in a fancy neighborhood out in Oyster Bay.

Mutchie is nervous all afternoon, so nervous that he finally has to buy Teresa lasagna at Luciano's to forestall a fight. By Monday morning, his mood has changed. It can't be true. Nobody in her right mind is going to sell a vintage racer for a fraction of its value, not even a lady named Morgan who got hers through a divorce. "The hell with her," thinks Mutchie. "But then," he says to himself and shrugs, "ya never know."

Teresa goes off to work while Mutchie is still reading the paper in the red silk dressing gown she bought him for Christmas. Fat Mutchie dithers around all morning. He picks a fight with his broker. He snarls at the cleaning girl. He hangs up on the crazy Haitian who's the super at his apartment building in Borough Park.

About noon, like in a dream, he gets Teresa's Mercedes from the next block and starts in the general direction of Oyster Bay. He stops for lunch. He gets lost. He stops for gas. He stops at a liquor store to ask directions.

Half-an-hour late, Mutchie finally rolls up to a pair of stone gate posts. Behind them is a driveway that Mutchie swears is "like the front straight at Bridgehampton, only smoother." At the end of this tree-lined private road is a building. "I figure I'm in the wrong place," says Mutchie. "Like maybe this is a private school or a rest home. I'm waiting for the guards to throw me out."

There's nobody around. Mutchie parks the Mercedes and punches the doorbell. A chime rings somewhere far away. Breathless Morgan answers the door herself. "The lady is gorgeous," remembers Mutchie with awe. "And she has manners you should think maybe she gives lessons to the Queen of England."

"I was afraid you weren't coming," says Breathless with a little pout. Mutchie settles into a Baroque wing chair—"real, not from Bargain Town." He sits there, breathing through his mouth. Breathless Morgan makes chit-chat for ten minutes, for twenty minutes, until Mutchie is wondering what the hell is going on. So finally he says, "Let's see the car."

They go outside. "There is a garage like I wake up at night and dream about," says Mutchie. "I could open a dealership in this garage, you'd never find it." The garage is empty. Except that way over in one corner, there is a car under a cover. Mutchie pulls the cover off.

"You're not gonna believe this," he tells me, "but underneath this cover is the best Morgan I've ever seen. It's to die for. This car...the engine is cleaner than the plates at Luciano's. The paint is better than on Teresa's Mercedes the day I bought it. The fenders aren't even cracked. This is a car comes along once in a lifetime, maybe not even then."

Mutchie wants this car so bad he can taste it. It starts right up. He helps Breathless into the passenger seat and they toodle off down the driveway. They drive around the neighborhood, and all the time Breathless is laughing and telling him how much she loves a car like this and how sad she is to sell it. She talks low, so Mutchie has to lean towards her till their heads are touching just so he can hear what she's saying over the exhaust.

He puts the Morgan back in the garage and covers it up. Breathless invites him in for "tea, or something a little stronger, if you prefer." Keeping careful not to spill his coffee on the Persian carpet, Fat Mutchie admits he lusts after her car, but he needs a day or two to get his affairs in order. "I must discuss this purchase with my associate," he says.

Mutchie's mind is racing like it's at LeMans. He can't let this car get away, and yet if he buys it, Teresa will kill him. Mutchie figures he will go home, he will make Teresa a nice plate of gnocchi with a little sweet Italian white wine to go with it, when she comes home from class he will soften her up and beg her to let him buy another Morgan. It's worked before; it shouldn't work again?

Breathless Morgan shakes Mutchie's hand, all the time giving his fingers little squeezes like a Victorian schoolgirl. She watches at the door when he drives away. By now it is getting dark. Mutchie finds a big Long Island grocery store and buys the stuff to make Teresa's favorite dinner. There is a discount liquor store down the row where he buys some wine.

When he gets back to the Mercedes, there is a flat tire on the left front. "Damn," says Mutchie. The spare is soft. He pumps up the spare at the gas station the other end of the mall. Then he changes the tire in the dark, getting grease stains on his hands and knees. On the way home, Mutchie gets lost in Queens. By the time he rolls onto Atlantic Avenue, it is midnight.

"I am not at this time exactly feeling like Gentleman Jim Corbett," explains Fat Mutchie. "I walk up the front stairs, and the door is locked. But the lights are on inside. What is this, I am wondering? We got company, maybe?"

Mutchie rings the door bell of his own house, and the cheap paper bag from the discount liquor store splits. The wine bottle smashes on the stone step.

Teresa opens the door. "Who the hell's Morgan, you two-timing jerk?"

"Whaddya, whaddya," says Fat Mutchie and drops the rest of his groceries.

"Your girlfriend called and left a message for you on the tape machine." Teresa talks in a sing-song parody of Breathless, like Madonna impersonating Mae West. "'It's after three,'" she sings. "'I'm looking forward to seeing you this afternoon. I hope you won't be too late.'"

"I went to see this lady about buying her car."

"A car! A car! What the hell do you need with another car? You liar. Is she pretty?"

"Yeah, she's beautiful," says Mutchie without thinking.

"Jerk!"

"She slams the door so hard," says Mutchie, "the cop on the beat thinks the kids are shooting off .38s in the park again. He wants to run me in for drunk and disorderly. I don't blame the stiff. It is now after midnight, I am myself covered with dirt, I am smelling like the floor of a saloon. That's when I get the cop to drop me at your house."

Fat Mutchie has been here three days, already. He is driving me crazy. He divides his time between eating, whining and calling home and talking to his answering machine, hoping Teresa will believe him sooner or later. Sometimes he eats and whines while he is on the phone, which can be very messy.

He is afraid to call Breathless. "She might still have the Morgan," he sighs, "and I couldn't resist to buy it. You shoulda seen this car. A once in a lifetime car, this was."

I ask him if he's learned his lesson. "Oh, yes," says Fat Mutchie seriously. "There is here a lesson for everyone. You're gonna buy some car, especially one your girlfriend ain't gonna like anyway, don't screw around. Buy the car. That way, at least you end up with something."

E Molto Difficile per un Pilote...Molto Difficile

The old man came to the track each morning, no matter how brightly the sun burned in the perpetually cloudless sky. Through the heat of the day he would sit motionless on the pit wall, erect as the bronze Garibaldi riding upon a pigeon-fouled horse in the town square.

Always he wore the same black wool suit, white shirt, black silk tie. His shirt collars turned up a little at the points, his mirror-polish black shoes cracked along the seams. No matter. He sat, tall and proud as an emperor, with his shriveled left leg sticking out awkwardly like a badly set wing on a hawk too valuable to destroy. Severe and monsignor-black he sat, only his eyes in motion.

The eyes! Hooded black eyes of the hawk, eyes that cut like a rapier. His hair was as full as ever, brushed straight back, though now gone completely white. The profile was still the same...hooked Caesar nose, pinched lips, taut cheeks...the skin as dry and yellowed as old newsprint. But all anyone remembered were the cold black eyes. And the livid scar.

The strong chin had a great scar that cut from the right corner of the mouth to the hinge of the jawbone on the opposite side. You could still see where the nervous young surgeon—dead decades ago during a shelling near Monte Cassino—had hurried his stitches, working in a ditch alongside the route of the Targa Florio, while peasants struggled to cut apart the remnants of the Maserati that still held his patient. What matter was the neatness of the scar when Pellegrino had already been given the Last Rites? *Nomine Pater, et Filius, et Spiritu Sancte...*

Pellegrino! *Pellegrino*! They had carried him through the streets of Brescia on their shoulders after the Mille Miglia, fifty thousand of them slicked down like seals by the cold rain, but warmed by the late hour, the cheap Lambrusco and the skill of Il Divino Pellegrino. They had carried him right into his hotel, right up to his laughing Isabella, her happy diva's eyes shining in the candlelight.

The mob feasted until the hotelier ran out of food and wine, and then they carried Pellegrino around the square again, singing the *Marcia Reale* in the rain while the people stood on their balconies under shiny black umbrellas and wept with excitement.

Another year after he had won in the broiling heat, they pushed him around the track at Monza, hundreds of them taking turns, pressing handprints into the aluminum tail of the Alfa Romeo. From the verge, two hundred thousand waved their arms over their heads and shouted *Pellegrino, Pellegrino* like waves slapping against the sand at Ravenna sur Mare.

His one extravagance was the curiously greenish-gold cane he absently caressed with his scarred old hand. The shaft had been machined from billet titanium by his long-time mechanic, Campagnoni, topped with the ivory shift knob from his favorite Maserati and engraved down the side *Commendatore Pellegrino Giorgio Leoni...Campionissimo del Mondo.*

They had presented it to him at a dinner in the ballroom under the Mayor's office in the town hall of Brescia. The Pretender King of Italy, a dusty little man with a dry cough and a red, white and green sash across his sunken chest, had held out his ring to be kissed. His ruby had seemed as large as the shift knob when Leoni had brushed the cold stone with his tight lips, and the crowd had climbed on their chairs to cheer.

And now he, Il Divino Pellegrino, spent his days sitting on a dusty concrete wall next to a race track. The track, it was nothing. A narrow ribbon of broken asphalt little more than 2 kilometers long, it wandered around in a series of vicious curves before disappearing behind a rocky hillock only to appear again on the far side, sweeping back to the meager pit lane where Pellegrino kept his vigil.

From all over Italy, from all over Europe, from all over the World, the pilgrims would come. They put up at the one small pensione in the tiny hill town, expecting the worst, and were delighted with the cool high-ceilinged rooms, the lean carpaccio and home-made linguine topped with white tartuffi, the thoughtful wine list, the dark-haired waitress with flashing eyes and breasts like melons. "This won't be so bad," they would say to themselves.

Over their espresso they would sit on the terrace in the dark and question the innkeeper. And he would give to all of them the same advice.

"To stand before Commendatore Leoni, this is easy. You must not go to his home, the farm that he has inherited from his mother's father. Nay. You will only anger him, and he has the temper of the very devil himself. But he attends early mass at San Carlo, here in our lovely Ronchesana, to pray for the soul of his beloved Isabella...diva Isabella Oreste of the Opera Milano. The angels wept when she died"—at this he wiped a tear from the corner of his eye—"but you have only to stand at the base of the steps, there, and he will see you as he passes."

At this point in his speech, the innkeeper would gesture solemnly toward the shadowy facade of San Carlo—a minor work by a student of Bernini—brooding fifty meters away at the other side of the square behind Garibaldi and his horse.

"He will see you, he will search you with his eyes of the hawk. But do not be disappointed if he does not speak with you. I have not left this square since my pappa died, eighteen years ago next month, bless his soul"—at this he crossed himself hurriedly—"and I have seen Il Pellegrino take only a handful of students. And with none of them was he satisfied."

The next morning, it would be as the innkeeper said. Pellegrino Leoni, leaning heavily on his cane, would slowly make his way down the sweeping Baroque steps after mass. He would search the faces of the young men and finding nothing, enter the back seat of an ancient Lancia Astura cabriolet driven by his dead wife's nephew's son. And he would be chauffeured the 15 kilometers to the track, his bad leg resting on the seat cushion next to him.

The track was owned by a rich industrialist from Milan, who had bought it many years ago when his son determined to be a racing driver like Pellegrino Leoni, and bring honor to himself, to his family and to Italy. Alas, the son had been cut in half by the hood when his Ferrari left the road near Firenzuola on the Mugello circuit.

The industrialist's frail wife, Paola, had cried and torn her hair, but he had merely paid for a daily novena and two marble monuments, one by the ditch where his son had died, the other at the practice track. He arranged for one of the boy's friends to rent what was now called Circuit Decimo, in honor of his son.

This friend, Carlo Lizzano, ran a school for aspiring racing drivers. He would fit them into cast-off driving gear and used helmets, then lead them quickly around the wicked little Circuit Decimo with its incongruous marble monument behind the flimsy wooden stands.

Lizzano had six old single-seaters, Taraschis, with Fiat components. He acted as his own mechanic. Rarely were more than two or three of these tired machines running at one time, but then rarely were there more than two students at Circuit Decimo.

Lizzano's school ran every morning, Monday through Saturday. Many of the students were novices, but many more were experienced drivers who wished to be seen by Il Divino Pellegrino, who hoped to demonstrate for him their skills. The rumor was that one word from Pellegrino, and a young driver could pick from any team...even, *Beate Maria*, that which bore the name of Commendatore Ferrari.

Afternoons, drivers who owned their own racing cars, or who had already acquired patrons to pay their bills, made the pilgrimage to this out-of-the-way track in the mountains. They explained to their suspicious wives and sweethearts that they had to go testing. Testing at a special place. What they really sought was a word from Il Pellegrino, a sign of encouragement, an acknowledgement that they had chosen the correct path. All went home disappointed.

For many years, Pellegrino had watched them, one after another, men and boys who thought themselves, wished themselves, to be racing drivers. Not in their own estimation, or that of their friends and patrons, or even in the eyes of the world, but in the black hawk eyes of Il Pellegrino.

There are two words Italians use when they refer to a racing driver. Most drivers are *corridore*. A few, a very few—perhaps one in a lifetime—are *pilote*...Nuvolari, Caracciola, Fangio, Moss, Leoni. Drivers who have crossed over the line, artists who can turn the pedestrian act of driving into a challenge of immortality. Men who have been marked by the gods for greatness. *Pilote*.

Pellegrino did not travel the world in search of treasure, but each day he searched, nonetheless. The world came to him, to Circuit Decimo. And he would patiently look into their eyes, into their souls, looking for that treasure, that spark of obsession that separates *corridore* from *pilote*.

When at last he found it, it was as though the gods had decided to play with Pellegrino, to amuse themselves by confusing an old man. He was sitting on the wall when his wife's nephew's son tapped him gently on the shoulder.

"Someone to see you, Commendatore."

It was himself. The boy—he could be no more than eighteen or nineteen—was the youthful Leoni. *Non Capisco!* Handsome as an angel, dark as a Gaul, with the same hawk's beak nose. He had the muscular yet compact build of a middleweight fighter, the sinuous muscles that had enabled Leoni to fight the wheel of wicked Alfas and Maseratis and yet never feel fatigue, that had let him get away with preposterous maneuvers that would have meant certain death to any other.

And the eyes! On the surface, the black eyes were lustrous, rimmed by long, almost girlish lashes. But when he looked into them, Pellegrino could see himself looking back. Pride. Arrogance. Fear. Obsession. The soul of a *pilote*.

"Where are your parents, my child?"

"My father, Eduardo Canestrini, owns this track, Commendatore. I am the younger brother of Decimo Canestrini, for whom it is named."

"And what is your name?"

"I am called Emanuele."

"Emanuele. Blessed of God. You must call me Pellegrino. Listen to me with your soul as well as your mind, and I will make you a god on earth...a *pilote*. A *pilote*...greater even than myself. For I, in my time, had no maestro to instruct me."

From that moment, the great Pellegrino and the young Emanuele were as inseparable as lovers. Isabella's nephew's son was relegated to cooking and cleaning for the two of them at the small ochre farm house, the color of an Etruscan vase, surrounded by vineyards and ancient stone walls. Emanuele took over his duties as chauffeur in the huge black Lancia.

Each dawn, the boy would accompany the old man to mass at San Carlo, then drive him to the shabby track. Through the heat of the day, Emanuele would circle the track in one of the Taraschis, while Carlo Lizzano labored to prepare another one for him to use when the overstressed car he was driving invariably failed. One corner at a time, one technique at a time, Emanuele was given the gift of all that Il Pellegrino had learned in a lifetime of racing.

Lizzano's Schola Decimo became a training camp for Emanuele, and the students who made the pilgrimage to Ronchesana were shamelessly enlisted by Pellegrino as sparring partners for his prodigy. Money, of course, was never a problem.

The Canestrini fortune was put at their disposal, over the objections of Emanuele's mother. She, rightly or wrongly, did not want to lose a second son in a racing car. Emanuele's father, rightly or wrongly, envisioned his son's unquestioned success as somehow settling his account with the gods of racing who had taken his first son from him.

The boy was a natural, as had been clear to Pellegrino from the start. Within weeks, he had outgrown the tired Taraschis. A matched pair of Maserati sports/racers were purchased, one for Emanuele, one for the ever-changing sparring partners, along with a truckload of spares and the services of a factory-trained mechanic.

A few of the more experienced corridore who

found their way to Circuit Decimo were initially faster than Emanuele in the Maseratis, but the gap quickly shrank. Within a month, the boy could race successfully against any opponent, even the teacher Carlo Lizzano, in matched cars.

A test day was arranged, in great secrecy, at Monza. A closed van from Modena brought last year's Formula Two car from Ferrari. The short Pista Junior course was used. Emanuele was carefully coached and brought up to speed gradually under the direction of Lizzano. By the end of the afternoon, he was within fractions of the factory drivers who had tested the same car here the year before. The day was proclaimed a great success and an arrangement was made for Industrie Canestrini SpA to lease a Ferrari factory team car for non-championship events.

Emanuele was proud, but appropriately humble. "The Blessed Father has given you back far more than he took from you," proclaimed Il Divino to Signor Canestrini upon their return to Rochesana, "I can see it in his eyes." The boy dropped his dark eyes with the girlish lashes in response, but it was only false modesty. In his heart, like Pellegrino, he held the arrogance of the hawk.

Signor Canestrini could not question the wisdom of so great a critic. But in the middle of the night, his soft-skinned, violet-eyed mistress Maria—who was also his confidante and private secretary—heard him call "Decimo" in a voice so anguished that she was unable to regain sleep and so appeared the next morning irritable and puffy-faced.

A minor Formula Two race on the Posillipo

circuit outside Naples was selected for Emanuele's debut. Signor Canestrini and Maria drove to Rochesana in her stylish black and silver Lancia Flaminia with the special body built by Pininfarina. They were to transport the prodigy south to Naples, along with his mentor.

They met at the Leoni farmhouse, under the weathered sign lettered *Casa Nostrum* that Isabella had affixed over the door as a bride. The day was hot and airless. Niccolo, Isabella's nephew's son, silently served them salad, fruit and pungent goat cheese, washed down with aqua minerale and harsh young wine. Conversation was as formal and stilted as that at a dinner party between two heads-of-state.

When it came time to leave in the late afternoon, Pellegrino would not accompany them. Emanuele pleaded, on the verge of tears, but Il Divino was adamant.

"I have taught you all that you need, Bambolo. I have seen too many races, and it tires my leg now to travel far from Rochesana. I will sit in the garden of my mother's father's house and await your success. You will return and tell me after you have won."

And like Monsignor Baghetti each morning at the doorway of San Carlo, like the King of the Vatican sending forth his legions to crusade against the Infidel, Pellegrino put his clawed old hand on Emanuele's head and gave his blessing.

"Do not be afraid to win."

"I am never afraid," shot back the boy. And with that he abruptly left the crippled old hawk sitting on a garden wall in the sun, his bad leg resting awkwardly on the hot stones.

Maria and Emanuele were of nearly an age, and so they spoke of the things which interest young people. The boy drove through the gin-clear night, Maria sitting in the front to help him stay awake and to read the map by the intimate greenish light of the instrument panel, while Signor Canestrini, sleepy from the wine and the heat, dozed in the back seat.

The three occupied a balconied suite at the old Hotel Belvedere in Naples, a sprawling Nineteenth Century pile famous for its kitchen and its view over the bay. Emanuele went to bed early, while Eduardo and Maria sat on the balcony late into the night, drinking brandy and espresso, watching the lights go out around the distant shore.

Snubbed up against the sides of a hill, Posillipo was a narrow 4 kilometers of up and down twists that followed trails stamped out in Roman times by cargo trains of asses. The broken pavement was edged by curbs and trees, walls and houses built right out to the road in the manner of all Italian hill towns.

Ignore the trees and the light posts, the curbs and the walls—all of which Pellegrino had taught him not to see as he was driving—and Posillipo was merely a longer version of his familiar Circuit Decimo, all wrist-wracking turns with no straight on which to rest.

The day was hot and dry, fatiguing to those who were not, like Emanuele, young and fit. He started from the pole, led every lap with fear and arrogance and won going away. The only moment of drama was near the end of the 30 laps, when he came to lap a tired back-marker from Firenza, one Guido Ferretti, driving an old Lancia-powered special assembled in his garage.

As Emanuele swung out to pass, the smoking Ferrettini darted towards him, darted back, mounted the curb and flipped into the post of a street lamp, throwing the driver against a wall. On Emanuele's next time around, a black-robed priest was performing the last rites over the broken body. By the last lap Ferretti had been removed and the car dragged out of sight behind a convenient hedge.

Signor Canestrini was ecstatic when the race was done, kissing Emanuele on both cheeks as they stood on the winner's podium. Maria shyly kissed his forehead and held his hand for a moment. He gave her the silver trophy, so large and ornate to compensate for the paucity of the purse that she had to carry it with two hands, as a mother might cradle a baby.

That night they dined at the Belvedere with business friends of his father's, fat men in dark suits who smoked evil little black cigars, drank too much wine and told coarse stories, after which they always looked at Maria, sitting quietly next to Emanuele, and said "Scusa, Signorina" before launching into their next ribald anecdote.

Emanuele left the table early, kissing Maria gently on the cheek and touching his father's shoulder. He ignored the fat friends of his father. He wanted to strike them; instead he gave a cold bow of insolence as he passed. He went to bed with a raging headache and woke with the stale stink of their cigar smoke in his nostrils still.

On their return to Rochesana, Emanuele left

his father and his father's mistress to lunch at the famous pensione. He himself drove the Lancia to Circuit Decimo. Il Divino was sitting in his accustomed place, balanced against the pull of his bad leg by his cane. The boy sat quietly next to him on the pit wall.

"So, Bambolo, I am told that things went well with you."

"Si, Commendatore."

Pellegrino raked him with his black eyes. "But you are not pleased. That is good. One must be hard on oneself if one is to succeed."

"Si, Commendatore."

Pellegrino searched him more closely. "Ah. It is that old fool Ferretti, in that sorry excuse for a car. If he chooses to throw himself on God's mercy in front of your eyes, that is no affair of yours. It is between the two of them. *Beate Maria Virgine*, *Beate Isabella*, pray for his soul." At this the old man crossed himself.

"Si, Commendatore. It is not Ferretti. He drove the car of his own will and took the risk. I accept that."

"Is it the girl? Maria? A beautiful girl to be sure, Bambolo, but no good can come from a woman who puts herself between father and son."

Emanuele blushed deeply. "Commendatore. It is not Maria. I swear. My father needs her far more than I do."

"That is wisely said." He laid his hand on the boy's arm. "If it is none of these things, then what is wrong?"

"It is hard for me to explain, Commendatore." He stared at his shoes. "I can see that I have some talent to drive fast the racing car. That I do not question. But I have the finest maestro in Italy. I have my own track. I have any car my father can buy. Does this make me a great *pilote*? Nay, Commendatore. I am nothing but a boy playing at cars."

Il Pellegrino turned his ferocious stare on this young fool. "*Idiota*. The gods have given you a gift that is beyond measure. It is given to very few men to be able to do something, anything, better than anyone else. You have this gift. Do you think Commendatore Ferrari, do you think Lizzano and your father, do you think I, *Il Pellegrino*, would waste our time if you had not this gift? I have waited twenty years for you. *Venti anno*."

"Si Commendatore. But what is the value of a gift except to he who receives it. And since I have not earned it, this gift is worth nothing to me."

"*Sancte Maria*. Who are you, Emanuele, to question the wisdom of Our Blessed Father? One has not the right to refuse such a gift. One must trust in the wisdom of God and use this gift as best he can. And in using this gift He has given you, you will be honoring Him."

"Nay, Commendatore. I do not accept this gift."

"You are not lacking in courage, Bambolo, if you will fight with God himself."

"One can take many liberties with God, and because he is God, in doing so even then will one be honoring Him."

Emanuele's black eyes were lustrous, rimmed by long, almost girlish lashes. But when he looked into them, Pellegrino could see himself looking back. Pride. Arrogance. Fear. Obsession. Yes. The great Pellegrino, *Il Divino*, had seen himself looking back.

He could see it clearly, now. The boy's eyes were not windows on his soul, but mirrors which had reflected what Pellegrino hoped to find there. He had thought to read the mind of the gods, and instead had been made to wear ass's ears.

Whom the gods would humble, they first make proud.

Emanuele left him then, driving slowly in Maria's Lancia back to Rochesana. He collected his clothes from the farmhouse, he collected his impatient father and his father's querulous mistress from the restaurant on the square, across from the church of San Carlo and the bronze Garibaldi. He drove back to Milan.

There was a terrific row with his father, of course, but his mother supported him. Maria left soon thereafter to find work in Torino. Nothing tragic happened to Emanuele, but he did not attain to greatness, either. One may take liberties with God, but one cannot expect Him to be pleased.

The old man came to the track each morning, no matter how brightly the sun burned in the perpetually cloudless sky. Through the heat of the day he would sit motionless on the pit wall leaning against the curiously greenish-gold cane he absently caressed with his scarred old hand.

From all over Italy, from all over Europe, from all over the World, the pilgrims would come. And he would patiently look into their eyes, into their souls, looking for that treasure, that spark of obsession that separates *corridore* from *pilote*. But all that anyone remembered were his cold black eyes. The eyes of the hawk.

E molto difficile per un pilote...molto difficile.

We'll Laugh Every Day

C*ool* was the word that summer. Dan Gurney was *cool*. Matt Lawson's new Mustang was *cool*. The Beatles were *cool*. But the *coolest* record was "My mother she once told me, don't love you any man. Take what he may give you, give of what you can." We knew a euphemism when we heard one... Miss Walker had taught us all about double-entendre and other cool stuff in English Composition.

Hey, *cool*, we bragged. If *I* met a girl like that, I'd give *her* what she could take. And then we'd grin as wolfishly as we knew how, and the guys would snicker, sitting there in the dark on the fenders of their cars. The lighted tips of our cigarettes reflected faintly on the empty beer cans stacked on the hood of Jimmy Madero's '55 Chevy.

I was working as a bag boy in a Grand Union in upstate New York, and had about as much chance of meeting A Girl Like That as I did of dating Jackie Kennedy. My best friend Mark was the gardener at the local Catholic church, at least until we both left for college in September. He called everything and everybody *cool*...so much so that it became his nickname. "Hey Cool," we called him, even his mother. He was going out to Indiana to learn to be a surgeon, and I was heading for Brown to be an engineer like my father. What I really wanted to do was design sports cars.

We'd labor six days a week to put money into our "education fund," liberate twenty bucks from our mothers' pocketbooks to take a high-school girl to the drive-in on Saturday night and have just enough left by Sunday to buy a six-pack of Carling Black Label and ten gallons of gas so we could drive around and get away from our parents and the dread Sunday Dinner.

Neither of us could afford a car *and* an education fund, so we had to borrow the family wheels. This was *not* cool, but what else could we do? Most of the time, Hey Cool's divorced mother let him have her Ford Falcon, metallic pickle green, three-on-the-tree. That prematurely-aged Falcon would do about 90 mph, flat-out, its little six-cylinder pounding just seconds away from cardiac arrest.

Every once in a while, her boyfriend Herb would lend us his baby blue Thunderbird, mostly to get us out of the house so they could be alone. The T-bird had wrap-around rear seats and front buckets divided by a console like a fighter plane's, so it was no good for dates. But it did have wire wheels and a 390 Police Interceptor V-8 that would show 120 mph on our favorite stretch of Route 9G, the only straight road in the county. That was *cool*.

Saturday nights, we'd double date in my father's Chrysler, a great white whale with roof-high tailfins and bench seats wide enough for teenage couples to lie down and squirm around. There was one night, just one, when I took the pretty blond checker from Register Five for a walk in the woods and left Hey Cool in the car with a pouty-lipped girl he'd met from a town across the river.

When Cheryl and I came back, they were both far too quiet, and they sat conspicuously apart in the back seat all the way home. The next morning, my father woke me up around noon to demand an explanation for the spots of blood on the hood of his Chrysler, and Hey Cool—who told me *everything*—never would admit what he had done with the pouty-lipped girl that night. I scrubbed all the way down to the primer before I got the dried blood out of that white paint.

In the spring, my mother had decided we needed a second car, now that she was working in a florist shop and I had to get to the Grand Union every day. My father and I shopped all the local foreign car places, and through some miracle, we sold her on a race-prepped Triumph TR-3 complete with rollbar, for just $1250. My mother was too short to see over the steering wheel, but I solved that problem by stuffing pillows under her until she stuck out of the Triumph like a little kid in a pedal-car.

The Triumph was Olde English Ivory, with a bright red, real leather interior, bucket seats and a floor shift. My friend Jeff had an Austin-Healey 100-6, and the two cars were just about evenly matched...the Healey was faster, the Triumph handled better over the patchy, frost-heaved two-lane blacktop that was the only test track we had.

One Sunday night in the beginning of August,

Hey Cool and I were out for our evening "breath of fresh air"...half-emptied six-pack on the floor of the Triumph, me slumped against the driver's door and driving slowly with one hand, Hey Cool dangling his right leg out the cut-down passenger door, his bare foot resting on the fender. He rode that way whenever possible, claiming it was cooler. Actually, he thought it was *cool*.

"This sucks the big one," he said, "hanging around this chickenshit town. I got a letter from Anna. She's got some problem, and she wants me to come see her in Maine before I go to college. Wanna go? She knows lots of cool girls for you."

Anna was a girl from our high school class who'd gotten herself a job working in a summer resort in Ogunquit. She and Hey Cool had gone steady for most of senior year, but they'd broken up when she told him she was going away for the summer. Now he said they were "just good friends." But when he was home alone, he also played Bob Dylan's "Don't think twice, it's all right" over and over, by the hour.

"*Cool*. Why don't we take the last two weeks and go. We deserve it, ya know."

"How we gonna do that, asshole? We haven't got any money, and we haven't got any way to get there."

"I don't know, we'll just *go*, that's all."

And we did. Just like that. Hey Cool's mother and Herb rented a vacation cabin at Lake George. Mom and Dad suddenly announced they were visiting my aunt in Indianapolis for the last two weeks of August. When I said I wanted to drive to Maine, I think they were happy that I wasn't going to be around the house without them to guard the place.

Hey Cool and I were each allowed to take two hundred dollars out of our savings accounts...that was three weeks pay. Anna told us about a campground right on the ocean at Well's Beach, and we liberated a bunch of camping gear from the basement of the Parish Hall where our old Boy Scout troop had it stored.

Still not believing our good luck, we found ourselves on the hottest Saturday morning in mid-August, driving along the Massachusetts Turnpike in a TR-3 loaded to the plimsoll line with two musty war-surplus tents, cooking gear, a Coleman lantern, suitcases, bedrolls, a bottle of Johnny Walker stolen from my father's liquor cabinet and Hey Cool's mother's portable radio. The Triumph had no radio, so we habitually drove with him balancing the portable on his knee...the knee that wasn't dangling over the door.

"I will never love you, the cost of love's too dear. But though I'll never love you, I'll stay with you one year." We grinned wolfishly, nudged each other in the ribs and started laughing until tears rolled down our cheeks. We had a hot sports car, money in our pockets and two weeks to do anything we wanted. And best of all, for the first time in our lives, our parents didn't know how to get in touch with us. We were *free*.

The overloaded Triumph could just about hold 110 mph if I kept my foot flat to the floor. Hey Cool amused himself by pointing wildly at the front wheels of the cars we passed poking along at the 70 mph speed limit. "Your wheels," he'd yell, waving his arm around and putting an exaggerated look of panic on his face. "Your *wheels*. They're *turning*!"

The driver would either ignore us completely—just some wild kids—or catching what he thought was the intent if not the actual message, would wave and pull off at the first rest stop to change his defective tire, thankful those nice young fellows had warned him before he had an accident.

After ten exhausting hours of rowing the Triumph through vacation traffic with the shift lever and listening to a raspy Stage IV exhaust accompanied by "Your *wheels*, your *wheels*!" I finally found our campground about suppertime. We paid for two weeks worth and picked a spot overlooking the Atlantic. I unloaded the car while Hey Cool stood on top of the nearest dune and took deep breaths of sea air.

We had both been Eagle Scouts, and before dark we had a campsite that looked like an illustration in *Boy's Life*. There were side-by-side pup tents, a driftwood fire inside a circle of rocks, and two picnic tables with benches dragged over from another campsite. One was the designated kitchen, the other was the dining room. When we were finished, we sat on the wet sand at the edge of the water, watched the stars come out and traded swigs of warm Johnny Walker.

The next morning, while Hey Cool swam off his hang-over in water that was cold enough to turn your ankles numb in seconds, I drove up to the highway where there was a little roadside stand dwarfed by a huge sign that said *Tourist Information*. A girl swung out from behind the counter as I slid to a stop in the gravel. I bounced over the cut-down door and unfolded myself.

"What a funny little car."

She had a teasing, low-pitched voice with just a hint of a downeast Maine accent, and bright blue eyes that flashed when they caught the sun. I'd never known that eyes could really *flash*. Those eyes looked me up and down without embarrassment.

"What a big fellow."

Thank God for Coach Williams. Against my will, Coach had exercised me for four years until I had the muscular thighs, broad shoulders and flat stomach that an all-conference running back needs. He had turned Hey Cool from a shy little kid into a ferocious interior lineman. If we had a hero, I guess it was Coach.

Her head didn't reach to my shoulder, and her white blonde hair was the same sun-bleached color as mine. It was pulled back in twin pony-tails, and I was sure she'd been a cheerleader. She was wearing a man's dress shirt with the tails tied around her waist and khaki shorts. We stood there in the hot morning sun for a long minute...memorizing.

"My name's Kate."

"Cool."

"You want a map or something?"

"What time do you get off work?"

"Where do you go to school?"

"Brown."

"I go to Simmons. I usually close down at 6."

She gave me a smile that flashed just like her eyes. I stood there with my mouth open, gasping like I'd just finished a set of wind sprints on a hot afternoon.

At 5:30, Hey Cool and I helped her lock the shutters for the night. We piled into the Triumph,

Hey Cool obligingly folding himself across the little back seat like an origami bear, and tore off to Ogunquit in search of Anna. Kate directed us to a Victorian gingerbread confection ringed by porches and topped by dormers. Peeling paint and rusted screens clearly spoke of better days.

Hey Cool disappeared to find Anna. We waited for a while, sitting on a porch swing. Then Kate and I walked the length of the beach and back, progressing from awkwardly holding hands and imagining what college would be like to discovering that we had read the same books and liked the way each other kissed. By the time we got back to the Triumph, we had already started a teasing kind of intimate banter.

I called her "Dear" or "Sweetheart" in the same flat tone my father used with my mother, and she called me "Honey" or "Darling" in a theatrically-overdone, sexy growl. By the time we found Hey Cool sitting on the ground by the car, we were stumbling with laughter, and I had more adrenalin wizzing through my system than I did the night we beat Arlington 31-30 on a screen pass with less than ten seconds on the clock.

"Where's Anna?"

"You know what Anna's problem is?" said Hey Cool.

"She can't live without you," I said. Kate and I giggled, intoxicated with ourselves.

"Asshole. Her problem is that she's pregnant."

"Oh my God." Kate put her hand on his shoulder, still clutching my hand with the other.

"Is it, uh...*yours*?"

"Jesus, you *are* an asshole. No, it's not mine. It's

Coach Williams'."

"Holy Shit. Wait'll my mother hears that." My mother was the president of the PTA.

"Wait'll Anna's father hears that." Her father was the president of the School Board.

"What's she going to do?"

"He's going to marry her. She said okay. That's what she wanted to tell me."

"What a bummer."

"Where is Coach now?"

"Coach Williams? You mean that wonderful example for our misguided youth? Our great leader? Our hero? *That* Coach Williams? He's been staying here all summer. He's working as a lifeguard down at York Beach. He'll be along to pick up his fiance any minute. That fucking asshole."

"How about a malt or something? I'm dying of thirst."

"Nah. You and Kate get something. I'm gonna walk home along the beach. See you kids later."

"Hey Cool...Mark...uh, like, I'm sorry."

"Yeah. Right."

The next day we spent at the beach. Hey Cool listened to the radio all morning..."We'll sing in the sunshine, we'll laugh every day. We'll sing in the sunshine, then I'll be on my way." They played that song every fifteen minutes...he didn't say anything, but I know it reminded him of Anna. Hell, it reminded *me* of Anna.

Then while I went body-surfing, he just marched out to where the biggest breakers crashed and he stood there. Hey Cool battled the ocean like a defensive lineman until half-a-dozen waves in a row tossed him under and he came up coughing and sputtering. He slept all afternoon, while I read *Road & Track*. Graham Hill had won the Monaco Grand Prix, there was a condescending road test of the new Mustang and a three-month-old In Memoriam for old Eddie Sachs and young Dave MacDonald who'd been killed at Indianapolis.

The sun was already low in the sky when we got back to our tents. Kate was sitting cross-legged on our picnic table, and she kissed me hello with an air of casual possession, like a long-married wife who knows her husband isn't going anywhere. We'd known each other twenty-four hours.

Sitting on the bench was another girl. She had long, dark hair, a pretty, round face and even concealed by an oversize sweatshirt that said *Holyoke*, what was obviously a great figure. Kate turned on her flashing smile.

"Hi Honey. This is Beth. We want to go to Old Orchard Beach."

Kate had to persuade Hey Cool to come along, but once he took a good look at Beth, he perked up a little. He and I ran through the showers and got dressed in record time. A TR-3 forces you to make friends pretty quickly. Beth was a head taller than Kate, and somehow, the only way she, Hey Cool and a four-point rollbar could all fit in the back seat of a TR-3 was if he put his arm around her shoulders, and she rested her bare legs across his lap. It looked like fun to me.

I drove with Kate snuggled up to my shoulder, kissing my ear and pinning my hand between her knees when I tried to shift gears. Old Orchard was an hour drive, and by the time we got there, I could see Hey Cool and Beth kissing in the rear-view mirror. Kate gave me one of her smiles, and winked. "And when a year is over, and I have gone away, you'll often think about me, and this is what you'll say..." Hey Cool never mentioned Anna to me again. Never once.

Old Orchard Beach was a turn-of-the-century resort town with a tacky main street, an amusement park and a full-time carnival. We made ourselves queasy on cotton candy, candied apples and the Whirligig of Death, won a couple of stuffed bears throwing footballs at milk bottles and stayed until they rolled up the sidewalks. Hey Cool and Beth were oblivious to everything but each other, and spoke to us only when directly addressed. Kate wore the same enigmatic smile I'd seen on the mother of the bride at my cousin's wedding.

"Can I drive your little car?" She hugged me closer and gave me the 240 watt version of her smile.

"Sure, I guess. But let me show you how."

So while Hey Cool and Beth made out in the back, Kate got my standard lesson in the intricacies of driving a Triumph with a racing cam that put all the power over 5000 rpm, a racing clutch like an on/off switch, a lightened flywheel that made and lost revs quicker than you could catch them and precise but heavy steering that required two hands on the same side in order to parallel park. It had taken my mother weeks before she could drive the TR-3 at all, and the reason I got to use it so much was that in her heart of hearts, my mother hated that car.

Kate caught on pretty quickly, and soon we were cruising down U.S. One, going maybe 60 mph. I had the radio and two stuffed bears in my lap. I laid my head back and looked up at the summer stars that seemed close enough to touch. I was just starting to count my blessings, starting with Kate, when a car came up behind us, *fast*, brights on, and skidded into formation about a foot behind our bumper. Then he tapped the Triumph to make sure we knew he was back there.

"Danny's such a shithead!" said Kate. "He must have followed us from Old Orchard."

"You know this asshole?"

"Yeah, it's my old boyfriend."

"How did he know you're with me?"

"This isn't exactly an invisible car, you know."

"Uh...how long ago did you two break up?"

"When did you come by the tourist office? Sunday? Yeah, Sunday night. I called him after you brought me home."

"You mean..."

"Yeah, Honey." She paused ironically. "You and me...it was love at first sight."

Hey Cool's lipstick-smeared face appeared between ours. "I don't mean to complain, but this asshole's lights are making my eyes hurt. And if he taps us again, those little chrome doodads Triumph calls bumpers are gonna be right here in the seat with Beth and me."

Kate glanced over her shoulder. "Hold on, kiddies."

She jammed the shifter into Third and floored it in a delicious roar of unmuffled exhaust, and the lights receded a few yards, only to come back to the bumper when she shifted into Fourth. Kate kept her foot down until the big Smiths speedo was pegging the needle at 120. The lights were still behind us.

"What's he driving?"

"Probably his father's Cadillac. Danny's old Ford won't go this fast."

Hey Cool's head poked up again. "Get off the highway. You can lose him on a winding road."

Kate ran a red light and slewed sloppily around a right-angle left-hander on to what was obviously the main street of a little town. *Kennebunkport* seemed to be the name on most of the stores. The whole town couldn't have been more than four blocks long...I caught a flash of a boatyard and masts in the harbor on the right, a white and yellow house covered with Victorian gingerbread on the left, and we were back in total darkness...except for a set of Cadillac headlights about fifty yards behind us.

The road began a crazy series of increasingly sharp left and right turns, running across surf-battered rocks along the edge of the ocean. Kate obviously knew the road, plunging into corners far beyond what her headlights revealed. It was all Second gear work except for an occassional straight stretch when she could click into Third. Hey Cool had one arm wrapped around the rollbar and the other around Beth's waist. He gave me a manic grin. Beth had her eyes closed. I think she was praying.

Kate's boyfriend in the Cadillac obviously had his hands full, because his headlights fell further and further back, until the Triumph suddenly veered sharply off to the right, between a pair of stone gateposts and up a narrow driveway that must have climbed for half a mile. At the end was a circle in front of a house that was about the same size as our high school. Even the white columns on the porch and the flagpole in the center of the lawn looked familiar.

"You can't wake him up at this hour," whispered Beth from the back seat.

"I can't, can't I?" The blue eyes flashed. "You just watch me."

"Kate..."

"Back in a minute, Darling." She hopped out, and ran around the corner of the house. A few minutes later, lights went on upstairs.

"What the hell?"

"This is Kate's grandfather's," said Beth.

"So?"

"So he's been pushing Danny at her since they were little kids. But if she asks him to, he'll just tell Danny it's over between him and Kate. At least for now."

"Just like that?"

"Kate's grandfather *owns* this county. If he told *me* to do something, *I'd* do it."

I switched seats while we waited, and when a quiet, subdued Kate came back, a Kate I'd never seen before, I drove us back to Ogunquit slowly, and in silence. There was no sign of Danny and the Cadillac...we passed no other car at all. She turned the late night Boston DJ off, tucked the radio under the seat and curled up like a little girl.

"Let's go watch the surf."

"Are you okay?"

Her smile didn't flash at all. She put her hand lightly on my arm. "Let's not talk about it, alright."

I switched off the ignition and rolled quietly down to our campsite. Hey Cool went into his tent and reappeared with a stack of blankets and a flashlight. He wordlessly led Beth by the hand into the dunes, while Kate and I followed, stumbling along in the dark. He stopped, handed me a couple of blankets, pointed to a depression in the sand and disappeared with Beth fifty yards down the beach. I could see the flashlight for a moment, before he flicked it off.

Next morning, the TR-3 refused to start. Bright sun, blue sky, 80 degrees and the starter just ground and ground. It took two quarts of oil to bring it back to Full on the dipstick, and when I pulled the plugs, the one from the Number Two cylinder was covered with little bits of shiny aluminum.

"Son of a *bitch*!"

Hey Cool poked his head out his tent flap.

"Something wrong?"

"Remember when Jerry holed a piston in his Ford? I think we just did the same thing."

"Kate missed a shift or two last night. By the way, how did you get her home?"

"She grabbed a shower and my best madras shirt and walked to work about an hour ago."

Beth's head appeared in the other tent flap. "You mean she never went home last night?"

"Neither did you."

"But my parents are in New York, and they don't care anyway. Kate's in big trouble."

"Aren't we all."

Hey Cool and I spent the rest of the morning fiddling with the Triumph while Beth slept. Eventually, we got it running on three cylinders without much more vibration than usual. The exhaust was blue and oily, but at least the thing ran. I cleaned and polished the body and swept the sand out of the rugs. Somehow, a clean car had always run better before. Besides, it gave me something to do.

At noon, I drove up to the corner to see Kate. She was next to me before I could get out of the car. She seemed smaller, prettier, more fragile...like my mother's favorite Dresden figurine...so finely-drawn it made your heart ache.

"Hi Lover. Am I glad to see you!"

"That shirt looks great. I would have come earlier, but we couldn't get the car going. I think we holed a piston last night."

"Is that bad?"

"It'll be okay. How are you?"

"Uh, well...my mom brought my clothes and stuff down here this morning."

"What?"

"It's no big deal. I can stay at Beth's. I have to leave for school next week, anyway."

"You can stay with me. Besides, Beth's here."

"Well, I guess I better stick with Beth." Her smile flashed, but the blue eyes stayed dull and scared. "I have to keep her out of trouble."

"*Cool*. But what if your grandfather finds out?"

"If we're lucky, Mom will be too scared to tell him...and we'll all have left for school before he finds out from somebody else."

We loaded her few suitcases in the Triumph, put the "Out to Lunch" sign on the Tourist Information counter, and coasted back down to our campsite. Beth—looking spectacular in Hey Cool's bathing trunks and his favorite T-shirt that said *Dan Gurney for President*—was setting the table. Hey Cool was cooking hamburgers over the fire, and I knew from experience that when he had his prized cast-iron Dutch Oven buried in the coals, he was baking an angel food cake. Hey Cool had been the best cook in our Boy Scout troop and his show-off dish was angel food cake.

While Kate told Beth about being thrown out of the house, I walked down and sat on the sand. Nobody was there except an old man clamming on the flats. The surf was way down, almost calm, and a line of seaweed barely moved at the edge of the water. The sun burned my eyes, even though I had my favorite Buddy Holly sunglasses with the dark glass and heavy black frames.

Friday night, I had been a virgin bag boy working in a Grand Union and living with my parents. It was only Tuesday morning, and now I was living in a tent on the beach with A Girl Like That, I had blown up my mother's car and for all I knew, Kate's grandfather was mobilizing the posse to hang me from the highest tree in Maine. That's if her boyfriend Danny didn't get to me first. I had just over a hundred dollars in my pocket, that had to last another week and a half.

As I walked up to our campsite, I could hear Hey Cool's mother's radio getting louder and louder.

"I will never love you, the cost of love's too dear,

"But though I'll never love you, I'll stay with you one year.

"We'll sing in the sunshine, we'll laugh every day,

"We'll sing in the sunshine, then I'll be on my way."

Kate met me at the top of the dune with her flashing smile. I scooped her up with one arm around her waist and the other under her knees. By the time I carried her to the lunch table, we were laughing so hard we couldn't stop. We laughed and laughed.

Don't Sweat the Small Stuff

Saturday, my best friend and I had driven to Maine from upstate New York for a vacation before we left for college. Sunday, I met Kate working in the local Tourist Information office. Monday, she fixed up my friend Hey Cool with her friend Beth. And she missed a shift and holed a piston in my mother's TR-3. And she broke up with her longtime boyfriend. And she spent the night with me. You couldn't say this girl didn't *live*.

Tuesday, Kate got thrown out of the house for not coming home the night before, so she and Beth moved in with Hey Cool and me, camping on the beach. This was all pretty potent stuff for a couple of New York farm boys who a week ago had thought sneaking a cigarette in study hall was about as exciting as life was gonna get. I could hardly wait to see what Wednesday would bring.

Wednesday brought an unsuspected domestic side of Kate. While Beth, Hey Cool and I spent the day at the beach, Kate put in eight smiling hours below her Tourist Information sign, hitched a ride into Ogunquit and came back with two bags of groceries. Then she cooked dinner, cleaned-up the campsite and did everyone's laundry.

When the three body surfers finally staggered home, sunburned, itchy, covered with sand and cranky, there was Kate...cool and freshly showered, exquisite in clean khaki shorts and her trademark man's dress shirt with the tails tied around her tiny waist. Tucked in her blond pony tail was a blue wild flower that matched the arrangement in a coffee can on the brightly-set table, and in her hand was a cheap Martini glass from the grocery store that matched the three next to the pitcher on the table.

"What the hell..."

"Hi, Honey. How was your day at the beach?"

Her hair was still wet when I kissed her.

"What's all this then?"

"Well...I wanted it to be nice tonight. I guess I'm feeling bad about Mom throwing me out. And I feel bad about hurting your car, and well...you know, everything." There was a long pause. "Uh...would you guys like a Martini?"

Kate slowly started to laugh, her sexy laugh that started with a flash of light in startlingly-blue eyes and ended with a husky growl that made me feel all twisted up inside. Before I met Kate, the only time I'd felt like that, Bruno Sammarco, Central High's All-State guard, had just put his helmet into my stomach with a closing speed of 20 mph. This time when I kissed Kate, Beth and Hey Cool had to find something else to look at.

After dinner, we brought our blankets down to the beach, and lay there counting the constellations and talking about college. Beth had to leave for Holyoke on Saturday, while the rest of us had until Monday to get ready for Freshman Orientation...Hey Cool leaving for Indiana, Kate for Simmons, me for Brown. You didn't have to be an egghead to figure out that we only had a couple more days before our lives were going to change in a big way.

"Honey, how bad is your Triumph?"

"Not bad," I lied. "Don't worry about it."

"I'm not worried, if you say so. But there's this wedding I have to go to in Boston on Saturday. We could bring Beth to the bus station, and I could go to the wedding..."

"Sure. We'll just have to take it slow, that's all."

Thursday, while Kate went to work, we got the Triumph going on three cylinders and drove Beth home. Her parents were in New York, and she still had to pack for school. Her parents' house turned out to be a huge, grey-shingled Victorian pile on the Ogunquit bluffs along the ritzy oceanfront path called the Marginal Way.

Beth made us drop her at the bottom of the driveway. Hey Cool and I offered to help her pack, but she told us with a kiss that we'd be more trouble than we were worth. Actually, she didn't want to have to explain us to the housekeeper, who thought Beth had been staying at Kate's house for the past week.

Instead, we decided it was our turn to do dinner. We putt-putted carefully down to the fishing docks at Perkin's Cove. For five dollars, we bought four huge lobsters fresh off the boat, and on the way home, corn and tomatoes from a farm stand.

At low tide, we took our war surplus entrenching tools down to the beach, and dug a bucket full of Little Necks. That and a couple of six-packs of Carling, and we had the best New England clam bake anybody could ever have. The only bothersome detail was that the Triumph's oil consumption was about 25 miles-per-quart, since it was being pumped right out through the piston top.

Friday, Hey Cool and I played mechanic. Short of a rebuilt engine, there wasn't much we could do, but we managed to drain the oil and some bits of aluminum, change the filter and fill the sump with straight STP. We figured that might slow down the oil loss. Then we washed and waxed the TR-3, on the well-proven theory that a clean car always runs better.

A TR-3 trunk is just about big enough for an overnight bag, if you squish it down. Friday night we strapped Beth's luggage all over the Triumph, using spare tent ropes to tie her suitcases to the rollbar, down the trunklid and over the front fenders, the way upstate hunters bring home a dead deer.

"We're gonna look like a band of Okies," said Hey Cool. "Boston or Bust!"

"Okies don't drive race-prepped TR-3s," I said.

"Yeah. And they don't drive already-broken race cars, either."

Kate and I tried to keep the conversation going at dinner, but Beth and Hey Cool were somewhere far, far away. We gave up early and went to bed. Curled together in my tent, we could hear them talking quietly, and then Beth started crying, softly. Eventually, she must have cried herself to sleep, because Kate and I were awake most of the night, and we didn't hear her again.

Saturday morning, we were all trying to be perky and friendly, so the others would feel happy. Kate was in what I had already come to recognize as her Dangerous Mood, when her eyes flashed in the sun, but without the laughter that usually went with them. Beth was always pretty quiet, deep and thoughtful...moreso today. Hey Cool was being crazy and silly, cracking jokes, pretending to wrestle with Beth's final suitcase, making us all laugh. But his eyes weren't smiling.

He had to lift Beth over her luggage and into the back seat, then vault in himself and scrunch down around the rollbar. Kate got in my driver's side, and sat half on me, half on Beth's suitcase. An anxious minute of grinding on the starter, a tremendous belch of blue oil smoke, and off we clattered on the high road to adventure...U.S. Route One.

Actually, it was better than we had any right to expect. I could keep up with weekend traffic, and aside from getting a lot of amused stares from the adults and catcalls from the kids, we had no problems. The poor broken and overloaded TR-3 just kept plugging along, its raspy open exhaust only a little more annoying than usual. We'd bottom the springs on bumps, and rub the tires on the fenders in the corners, but as Hey Cool always said, "Hey Cool, don't sweat the small stuff."

The Triumph stopped just after we crossed the border into New Hampshire. I mean, it *stopped*. Even with our limited mechanical knowledge, Hey Cool and I could tell this car was not going to move another foot under its own power.

"How bad is it, Honey?"

"Well, you hear that rattling down in the bottom when I turn it over? I think that means we sawed the crankshaft in half."

"Is that bad?"

"No, not too bad. Don't worry about it."

"Naw, don't sweat the small stuff, Kate," said Hey Cool. "On a full-race engine like this, it's nothing that $2000 won't fix."

"Honey, I had no idea!"

I gave Hey Cool my best wolfish grin. "Thanks, asshole," I said. "Why'd you have to upset Kate. It's not really her fault. It just happened."

"Yeah. It just happened...when she downshifted at 8000 rpm."

"So what're we gonna do?" It was Beth reporting in from the back seat, somewhere beneath a stack of luggage. "I can't hitch to Boston with all this shit."

Hey Cool put on his most extravagant mock-British accent. "Simple, my dahling. Leave evahrythang to *moi*. We'll simply ring up the taxi queue round the cawnawh."

Kate ignored him. "Honey, can we rent a car?"

"Uh, why...uh, sure. Why not. My father gave me his credit card...just in case."

Beth and Hey Cool stayed with the Triumph while Kate and I alternated walking in the hot sun and hitching in a series of cars that all seemed to be '57 Fords with rusted-out mufflers. None of them were going more than a block. I was wearing my favorite Madras shorts, a blue dress shirt and my Bass Weejuns with no socks. And my Buddy Holly sunglasses with the heavy black plastic frames. This was a pretty dressy outfit for me, in mid-summer.

Kate was dressed for a wedding, which meant

a short skirt, scoop-neck dress made of some sort of white silk brocade, white stiletto heel slingbacks and a white bow in her shoulder-length hair. Passing motorists looked at us pretty curiously as we hitched along the Route One verge, particularly after Kate took her shoes off so she could walk.

The Hertz Lady had a bouffant hairdo with a pinkish rinse and blue-framed eyeglasses that swept up to harlequin points. There was a rhinestone in each point. She emphatically did *not* want to rent a car to a pair of sweaty and disheveled eighteen-year-olds. She obviously thought my father's credit card was stolen. She didn't want to let us talk to her supervisor.

Finally, it turned out that Kate knew her younger sister from Simmons, and after half-an-hour of alternately flashing her smile and her eyes, Kate talked the Hertz Lady into renting us a brand-new, 1964 Ford Galaxy 500 with 941 miles on the odometer. I had to leave her $100 for a cash deposit, which left me exactly nine dollars in my pocket. I didn't want to think about what my father was going to say..."*Renting* a car to drive to Boston? Whatsa matter, you too grand for the bus, college boy?"

"I thought you were a freshman?"

"I am."

"Then how'd you know her sister?"

The blue eyes shone dangerously. "I don't. I made it all up. But people *want* to believe you...don't you know that. What a dope...and that hairdo. Ugh." She gave me her top-grade smile, the one that combined both flashing blue eyes and sexy laugh. "Besides, we got the car, didn't we?"

After the tiny TR-3, the Galaxy 500 felt wider

than the road...a great flaccid animal undulating down U.S. One. It was a white four-door, with a red vinyl interior. I had all I could do to keep the bulbous fenders in the lane, knuckles wrapped tight around the thin plastic steering wheel. Ford had thoughtfully provided a chrome gunsight on each fender I could use for aiming this beast.

Kate sat leaning against the passenger door, with her legs across the bench seat and her bare feet resting on my thigh. She tuned the radio to WBZ in Boston. The Beatles were singing "I wanna hold your hand, yeh, yeh, yeh, yeh."

"I wanna hold your foot," I sang, tickling her bare feet. "Yeh, yeh, yeh, yeh."

"Creep. Cut it out!" But she was laughing, and she crawled over and gave me a big wet kiss on the ear. "There... take that."

Hey Cool and Beth were not in such a good mood. Sitting beside the highway in a broken down convertible on a hot sunny day is not guaranteed to improve a relationship. Kate gave them bottles of Coke from the Hertz office vending machine. The Cokes didn't help much.

"Where the hell have you two been? Beth is gonna miss her bus."

"So? Kate's gonna miss that wedding. My mom is gonna miss her car. I'm *not* gonna miss a ration of shit from my father. Everybody's got problems today. What happened to The One and Only, Imperturbable Mr. Cool?"

"Cool, like...I'm sorry, you know. This is my last day with Beth and well...you know."

"Hey Cool...Mark...I know."

"Help me load Beth's stuff in this boat. Did you

guys have trouble or something?"

"Nothing Kate couldn't handle. She just invented The Old School Tie. These New England preppies stick together, you know." Kate gave me her wicked smile. And The Finger.

"What the hell is this thing, anyway. A Galaxy 500?" Hey Cool popped the hood. "Hey look. It's got the same engine as Herb's T-Bird. It oughta go 120, easy. We might still make Beth's bus."

"First we've got to tow the Triumph about five miles down the road. The dopey Hertz Lady said that's the only foreign car place in this whole area. Help me hook up these tent ropes. You'll have to steer and brake. Just like that time you and Anna got stuck in the mud out in the woods and I had to come rescue you. Remember? Your mother never could figure out how you got her Falcon so dirty at a high school dance."

"Yeah, right. Anna was another lifetime. BB. Before Beth."

Of course, Jerry's Foreign Car Service was closed. It was Saturday afternoon in late August. We pushed the TR-3 in front of Jerry's overhead doors, with a note under the windshield wiper written with Kate's lipstick on a page ripped out of the Owner's Manual. It was the first page of the chapter that told you how to rebuild the engine.

Hey Cool and Beth fooled around in the back seat of the Galaxy, giggling and cuddling. Kate again leaned against the passenger door, feet on my thigh, softly singing along with the radio, eyes closed. I cut across to the New Hampshire Turnpike, where the big Ford could happily hold 100 mph on its funny ribbon speedometer.

The Galaxy was quiet enough to listen to the radio even with the windows down, all Beth's luggage fit in the trunk, the four of us fit in the interior with room to spare, and after a week of being pummeled by a topless, racing Triumph with an open exhaust, the Galaxy seemed like the softest, most luxurious sedan we'd ever been in.

Compared to my father's Chrysler, it was a handful...soft and flabby, with vague steering. It weaved and wandered in the lane, and took a lot of concentration to hold straight. Going through the tunnel under Boston Harbor near the Navy Yard, I could swear I was going to scrape the curved tunnel roof. The congested lanes of Boston traffic seemed about *this* wide.

Kate and Beth knew their way around Boston, otherwise Hey Cool and I would still be there riding in circles, like Charlie on the MTA. We didn't have anything like Boston traffic in upstate New York. Hell, the worst thing we had to worry about at home was coming over a blind hill and finding a John Deere towing a trailer full of cow manure at 5 mph. In Boston traffic, I felt like a big white cue ball in a giant game of billiards.

We got Beth to the bus station with ten minutes to spare. Hey Cool and I carried her luggage out to the platform, while Kate stayed with the Galaxy in a No Parking Zone and Beth bought her bus ticket. I kissed Beth quickly goodby, and went back to wait in the car while Hey Cool said goodby properly. He was unexpectedly happy when he came out.

"Beth is gonna come see me next month at school. And we can get together at Christmas. And I'll come to Ogunquit next summer."

He crowded into the front seat with us, and we steamed off to Beacon Hill to find the wedding reception...Kate had already missed the wedding itself by hours. The reception was in one of those Colonial red brick townhouses, with white trim, set on a pretty square planted with flowering trees. A wrought iron fence kept out the riff-raff, and the street was actually made from cobblestones...the first cobblestone street I'd ever seen.

Kate kissed me, hopped out at the curb, slipped her shoes on and ran up the steps to the brightly-varnished front door. She turned and smiled at us as she zipped inside.

"She sure is something else." It was the first time Hey Cool had ever said anything like that, about Kate or anyone else I'd ever gone out with.

"Yeah. So's Beth."

"Beth is great, but Kate is so...*alive*. She's like a child, or a wild animal or the wind, or something."

This was pretty poetic for an offesive tackle. "Do you remember Bobbie Jean?"

"Sure. No more brains than a tray of ice cubes, but the best french kisser in three counties. What the hell made you think of Bobbie Jean?"

"Oh, nothing. How far we've come, I guess. I mean, there's a pretty big difference between Kate and Bobbie Jean."

Bobbie Jean Paulding was Hey Cool's steady girlfriend before he met Anna. Well, actually it's more complicated than that. Hey Cool and Bobbie Jean had gone steady for about a year. Then they had a big fight, that came to a head one afternoon in mid-winter. We'd just driven home from school in Hey Cool's mother's Falcon...we always came home as late as we could get away with, so we'd have to spend less time at home. It was almost dark, it had just started to snow. The two of them stood in the road, screaming at each other like, well...parents.

I was trying to play moderator. As ironically as I could, I said to Bobbie Jean, "So, what are you doing Friday night?"

I expected Hey Cool would say something along the lines of "You asshole, she's *my* girlfriend." And we'd all laugh, and they'd realize how much they liked each other. Instead, Hey Cool turned and walked away into the snow, leaving me standing there in the icy dirt road with Bobbie Jean.

"Going out with you, I guess."

I was trapped. And I didn't even like her all that well. But for the next year, Bobbie Jean and I went steady, until she started dating Karen Braman's brother, Kenny, who was two years older than us, slicked back his hair with Brylcreme, went to the local Junior College and drove a Plymouth Valiant with a push-button shifter in the steering wheel hub. What a geek. When Bobbie Jean broke up with me to date Kenny, I wasn't hurt, I was *insulted.*

Throughout that year, though, Hey Cool and I were never not Best Friends. And it was only because I was going with Bobbie Jean that he had been able to meet Anna. And Anna was the reason we were in Maine at all. She'd dragged Hey Cool all the way to Ogunquit to tell him she was going to marry somebody else. And have the guy's baby. But then we'd met Kate and Beth, and like Hey Cool said, Bobbie Jean and Anna had happened in another lifetime, far, far away.

We sat in the Galaxy for hours, listening to

WBZ AM, talking about girls, what college would be like and what it must be like to be rich, like Kate and her friends. We took a walk around the block in the gathering dusk, and looked at the cars. There were the expected rows of big American cars, Cadillacs and Chryslers with roof-high fins, but also two Mercedes, a Renault R-8 and a handful of cars I'd only seen in pictures in *Sports Car Graphic*. Our favorites were a green Elva Courier, a white Lancia Aurelia and a dark blue Bentley Continental Flying Spur that simply ached of elegance far beyond anything we had ever imagined.

When Kate finally found the Galaxy in the dark, she was carrying her shoes in one hand, along with a bottle of Mumm's Cordon Rouge. In her other hand was another bottle of champagne. Her hair was a tangled mess, all down in her eyes, and she was laughing out loud, great bellows of laughter that echoed off the brick townhouses. She turned and called over her shoulder to a shadow wobbling along behind her.

"Come *on*, Re-Re. The guys are over here."

"Honey, this is Marie. We call her Re-Re. Isn't that cute? She needs a ride home to Portsmouth."

"You're drunk."

"Of course I'm drunk. I've been drinking champagne. I brought some for you."

"But I have to drive."

"Well screw you, then. Come'on Re-Re. We'll find somebody else to take us home. Somebody who isn't too stuck up to have a drink or two."

"Hey Cool, help me get them in the car before somebody calls the cops."

I grabbed Kate around the waist, but she twisted

away. She started down the sidewalk, but Hey Cool opened his arms and scooped her in, just like he would a running back who ventured too near the line of scrimmage. He picked Kate up, carried her over to the Galaxy, and simply tumbled into the back seat with her in his arms.

Re-Re started running down the cobblestones, yelling. I grabbed her from behind, ducking a blow from yet another Mumm's bottle. I picked her up with one arm around her waist—she was even thinner and lighter than Kate—and tossed us both into the driver's door of the Galaxy. I slammed the door, started the engine, switched on the headlights and shifted the column automatic into Drive, all with my left hand. My right arm was around Re-Re's waist. A wild swing with her half-empty bottle sprayed us both with Mumm's...not to mention, most of the Ford's interior.

Re-Re could have been Kate's sister...even with smeared make-up and champagne stains on what was obviously a horrendously-expensive white silk dress, she was a knockout. Her strawberry-blond hair was waist-length and no doubt had been carefully-ironed, Mary Travers style. She struggled against me until the Galaxy was up to speed, then looked around, kicked off her high-heels, sighed, kissed me full on the mouth, smiled, stretched out on the bench seat and nestled her head on my hip. All without spilling her champagne, which she managed to keep drinking from the bottle without moving her head from my hip.

I looked in the rearview mirror. Kate was entwined around Hey Cool, drunkenly kissing him. When she came up for air, Hey Cool took a swig from her champagne bottle, lifted the bottle in a toast and said huskily, "To Bobbie Jean Paulding...she loved not wisely, but two men." Then he gave me his best wolfish grin into the rearview mirror. "And to the two men who loved her, not wisely, but real well."

I wandered around Boston for half-an-hour, looking for a highway entrance. Hey Cool and Kate were now lying on the back seat, making out. Re-Re pulled my right hand off the wheel, and held it in both of hers until I started to stroke her hair and cheek.

Once I finally found the highway, I held the Ford at a leisurely 75, and cruised north in the dark, listening to WBZ's Late Night Music for Lovers and casually petting Re-Re under that ruined silk dress. Every once in a while, Kate would giggle in the back seat, and my stomach would turn over. And Re-Re would reach up and kiss me again, and then settle back in my lap.

She didn't notice when we passed the Portsmouth exit off the highway, so I just kept going. It was almost dawn by the time I quietly rolled up to our campsite in Well's Beach...the horizon over the blue-black ocean was already turning pink and gold, way out to sea, and the first gulls were just taking off against the lighter blue of the sky. The wind was off the ocean...it would be a perfect day at the beach.

Hey Cool and Kate were sound asleep in the back seat, and Re-Re made only the smallest little girl sleep sounds when I slid out the door and lowered her head off my leg and onto the seat. I quickly showered and shaved, changed my clothes and packed all my personal belongings in the Galaxy trunk. I was planning to be out of there by myself, as soon as I could get the rest of them out of my car. I slammed the lid when I shut it, hoping to wake up Kate and Hey Cool.

It was like the best magic trick I've ever seen. I slammed the trunk, and simultaneously, two lipstick-smeared faces appeared in the back window, eyes blinking in a golden shaft of sunlight that broke through the dawn horizon like the Judgement of God. And at the same time, like he'd been practicing it for months, my father's Chrysler rolled to a stop in front of the Galaxy, high-beams glaring.

Hey Cool was out of the car in a flash, trying to look as though meeting my parents at dawn on the beach in Maine was perfectly normal. The effect was partly spoiled by his pants, which were still around his knees and tackled him as he came through the Galaxy door. Kate was only seconds behind him. She was still pulling her skirt down as she swayed against the fender, trying to focus in the bright sunlight.

Re-Re sat up, slowly, snatched at her tangled hair in the rear view mirror, slid out the driver's door, adjusted her clothes, looked around until she found me standing behind the Galaxy with my hands still on the trunk lid and called loudly enough to wake the whole campground, "Who the fuck are these assholes, anyway. Not cops. I hate cops." Then she threw up, kneeling next to the front wheel of the Galaxy.

"Hi, Mom. Hi, Dad. What're you doing here?"

"Your father is so mad he can't speak. American Express called him to approve your use of his card. We thought you might be in trouble, so we called the very nice lady in the Hertz office who helped you out. She gave us this young lady's name, and we talked to her mother. Who is very upset, I don't suppose I have to tell you."

My mother looked at Re-Re in disgust. "What do you have to say for yourself, young lady? Katherine, I'm speaking to you."

"Uh, Mom. That's Marie. Kate's over here." Kate now had both arms around Hey Cool's neck, trying to stay upright. He had one arm around her waist. When my mother glared at them, Hey Cool gave her this silly little wave with his free hand. "Morning, Mrs. T," he said. "How you been?"

My mother was a sniffer. She now sniffed in her snootiest way and looked down her nose at us. "Why don't you children get cleaned up and we'll take you home." This was what Miss Walker had taught us is called a rhetorical question. Also known as an order.

While Kate and Re-Re scampered to the showers, Hey Cool and I packed everyone's stuff in the trunk of the Chrysler. We were being careful not to look at each other, shuffling back and forth with our heads down.

Finally, I whispered, "How could you?"

"Remember Bobbie Jean? How could *you*?"

"But I never knew you cared."

"You never asked."

Cleaned up and wearing identical outfits—one of my dress shirts, a pair of Kate's khaki shorts and a pony tail tied with a schoolgirl bow—Kate and Re-Re looked like twins...quiet, shame-faced, nauseous twins.

We waited while Hey Cool showered and changed. My parents continued to sit in the Chrysler, rigid with disgust. Re-Re lay down on the picnic table and closed her eyes. Kate came over to where I was staring out to sea, seeing nothing, and slipped her arm through mine.

"Honey?"

"What do you want?"

"Honey, I'm sorry. I was drunk, and well, it just happened. I'm sorry."

"But how could you? What about Beth? She's your friend. Hey Cool is my friend."

"And I'm your friend. Honest. And I'm really sorry. Can't we just forget yesterday ever happened?"

"Try that on my father."

"I don't care about your father. Or Hey Cool. I care about you." She kissed me so long I ran out of breath. Her eyes really were blue. And they really did flash with light.

Hey Cool and Re-Re sat on opposite sides of the Chrysler's back seat, with my non-speaking parents in front. Kate rode with me in the Galaxy, holding hands. After we returned the rental car, she sat in the back seat next to Re-Re, while I sat in the front with my parents. My mother put the hundred dollar deposit in her purse. Nobody said a word. Not one word.

An hour later, we dropped the two girls at Re-Re's house in Portsmouth, with only seconds for a quick hug goodby. For Hey Cool and I, penance was a painfully silent, eight-hour ride to upstate New York with my parents. When he got out of the car, Hey Cool winked at me.

"See you around, Cool," he said.

"Yeah, see you at Christmas. Uh, you know,

like...I'm sorry I never asked."

"Be cool about Kate, you know what I mean."

"Yeah. Don't sweat the small stuff."

The next day, still not speaking to me, my parents drove me to Brown, six hours away, in Providence. That evening after they finally left, the first thing I did was call Kate.

Great Uncle Brotherton

In those days, freshmen at Brown University were not allowed to have cars on campus. No problem. If we park two blocks away, argued Jason, then the car won't really be *on* campus, because it'll clearly be *off* campus. Todd and I could see the logic of that. And so we started looking for a car we could afford. Aye, there's the rub.

My two freshman roommates were a Waspy engineer from New Haven named Chesterton Todd Ward, IV who was chronically shy with girls but could do calculus in his head and a Jewish musical prodigy from Long Island named Jason Mildstein who had a stammer—"B-B-But only wh-wh-en wh-when I ge-get excited."

We were all on scholarship, and between the three of us, we figured we might scrape together a hundred bucks for a car. Even in 1965, this was not a lot of money. In a month of looking, we didn't find anything that even came close to our budget.

And then Todd's Great Uncle Brotherton died.

Todd went home to New Haven for the funeral and stayed to help his mother tidy up the old man's affairs. As it worked out, that weekend Brown was playing Yale at the Yale Bowl, so Todd agreed to meet Jason and I if we took the train from Providence to New Haven. We could stay with his parents.

Todd's parents were camping out at Great Uncle Brotherton's, an absolutely gigantic Victorian pile set in the midst of its own park in the center of New Haven. It was crammed to the window sills with stuff. Some rooms were literally impossible to walk into they were so strewn with furniture, books, clothes, quilts...you name it and Great Uncle Brotherton had one, two, probably a collection.

Todd's mother was one of those ethereal types...pretty and pale, but with a distracted air and a wisp of blonde hair perpetually out of place. She was sorting the really valuable antiques from the run-of-the-mill antiques, which meant she stood in the hall while Jason, Todd and I staggered back and forth carrying Victorian furniture that weighed enough to be cast from solid lead.

Soon Mrs. Ward was dividing it into three piles...Really Valuable Antiques, The Boys' Room At Brown and Everything Else. By the time we were finished around midnight, "The Boys" had collected an impressive pile of chairs, tables, quilts, books and lamps in return for our work.

"Well, I guess that's about everything," sighed Mrs. Ward, brushing a wisp of hair out of her eyes and leaving a dirty fingerprint across her forehead. "Except for Great Uncle Brotherton's car. I just don't know what to do with that."

"C-C-Car?" stammered Jason. "What k-kind of c-c-car?"

"Oh, just an old car that Uncle bought many years ago in England. It's still in the garage, I should think. It hasn't been run in months, though it does have license plates. He made me go down to the motor vehicle office with him just a month ago."

Then she started to sniffle at the memory, and Todd walked her gently into the living room and sat her down on an overstuffed sofa that looked like something rescued from a Mississippi stern-wheeler's casino.

Jason beat me to the door by a footstep, but we were flat even when we reached the garage. We yanked open the creaking old door, pushed a stack of yellow newspapers out of the way...and stopped dead in our tracks.

"What the hell?"

"It must b-b-be t-t-thirty years old."

It was dark green. "British, I'd guess," I said sagely. I was the car expert.

"I k-k-knew, I kn-knew that. Mrs. Ward said he b-b-bought it in England. Re-re-member? B-B-ut what is-*is* it?"

Jason got a flashlight from the kitchen and ran back outside again. By now I had crawled up to the front. At the top of the radiator was an elaborate enamelled emblem, a capital "I" bracketed by multicolored wings. Down the "I" was spelled out I-N-V-I-C-T-A.

"It's an Invicta."

"W-W-hat's that?"

"An old British car."

"I k-k-new kn-knew *that*."

My grandfather had gone through a collection of similarly expensive British cars—all now long gone. He had taught me how to drive some of them as a child. I clambered back over the front fender, past the sidemount and the outside brake lever, stepped over the doorless side of the body and slid down behind the four-spoke steering wheel...putting the rightside gearshift up my pant leg.

Once I got that straightened out, it was just like any of my grandfather's early Bentleys, Royces or Daimlers...spark and throttle levers on the steering wheel hub, starter button on the dash. In the weak yellow glimmer of Jason's flashlight, I diddled around with levers and buttons until a noisy mechanical clattering blew out the hood vents, followed by a heavily muffled *whuff, whuff, whuff* from the exhaust.

There was a big lock-out lever on the shifter that let you get into reverse, and a metal gate for the gears. It slicked in with no effort, and I jerkily backed out, narrowly missing an Empire Armoire and a box labelled *china* in shaky crayon. I stopped in front of the house and found the headlight switch.

"Is Monsieur perhaps going my vay?"

"Wh-What?"

"Get in."

Jason snuggled into the tan leather bucket seat and I burbled off down the driveway. It wasn't a driveway really, more like a private road that wound around the property for a mile or so. We did a couple of slow laps, cutting through piles of red and yellow leaves that were already starting to accumulate in early October. It was cold enough to see your breath.

Jason wiped his runny nose on his sleeve as we came into the warm living room. "Uh-uh Mrs. Wa-Ward. W-Would you li-like to-to s-sell th-that c-c-car?"

Todd's mother wasn't yet used to Jason's speech patterns. "What did he say?"

I translated. "Jason and I would like to buy Great Uncle Brotherton's In-In-Invicta." Now he had *me* doing it.

"Do you know what it's worth?"

I wasn't going to lie to her. "Well," I offered dubiously. "We have a hun-, a hun-, *damnit*, a hundred dollars."

We waited breathlessly to see what she would say. She brushed the hair out of her eyes, again. "That seems like an awful lot of money for such an old car. Why, it doesn't even have a top. But if you boys really want it...how about fifty dollars. That will leave you something for gasoline to drive back to Providence. The insurance is already paid through the end of the year," she pointed out encouragingly.

Jason and I solemnly counted out twenty-five dollars each from our wallets and presented it to Mrs. Ward, successfully resisting the urge to nudge each other in the ribs and laugh out loud until we were back outside. Then we carefully rolled the Invicta, *our* Invicta, back into the garage for the night.

Saturday morning we were up early, cleaning and polishing our new find. We checked the oil and generally busied ourselves fiddling with things while the Wards slept in Great Uncle Brotherton's dusty feather beds. There was a bunch of papers in the pretty wooden-fronted glovebox.

"Th-This c-c-car was b-built in 1933," read Jason, leafing through the owner's manual. "It h-h-has a 4.5-liter Me-Meadows engine, underslung ch-chassis and b-body by C-C-Carbodies, Ltd. It c-cost Uncle B-Brotherton $3775. It's c-called a Type S Tourer. Gee, t-that was a lot of m-money in 1933."

Todd strolled down around noon, regally dressed for the Yale game in a raccoon coat of Great Uncle Brotherton's that obviously dated from when the Invicta was young. He had thoughtfully brought discarded topcoats for Jason and I. He hopped in the back seat and breezily gave us directions to his high-school girlfriend's house. This was an unexpected side of Todd...Jason and I had never seen him even *speak* to a coed.

The girlfriend turned out to be a perfectly pleasant blonde from UConn, only slightly put-off by having to wear an old man's tweed coat and sit in the icy 60 mph hurricane blowing through the rear seat of a 4.5-liter Invicta Tourer. We performed a ceremonial tour around the Yale campus before heading out to the game. There was scattered applause from the peasants. Brown lost to Yale, again.

Sunday afternoon, nursing splendid hangovers from a party with some of Todd's friends at Yale that lasted until breakfast, Jason and I contemplated fitting a quart of furniture into a pint of Invicta. We finally ended up lacing furniture in various strategic locations over the rear fenders, then tying more on top of that. Todd had to squeeze into the rear seat by removing the raccoon coat, sliding down inside some table legs, then having us drape the coat over him like a traveling robe.

We took local roads all the way to Providence.

The air was positively golden, crisp but not cold, and the New England fall foliage was just at its tourist-luring height. Wrapped in one of Great Uncle Brotherton's ancient camels hair topcoats, I sat like Donald Healey behind the block-long hood of the Invicta, the top of the steering wheel even off with my nose, deftly snicking up and down through the gears, sawing away at the wheel, listening to the roar of the exhaust on the overrun. I was having the time of my young life.

We unloaded outside our dorm on a typically-quiet Sunday night, then I sneaked away to a parking lot on the other side of The Hill. Monday, Jason found us a parking spot in a nearby garage for ten dollars a month, and that night, he and I parked the Invicta safely away from prying eyes.

We soon fell into a routine. Every Friday afternoon, we'd clean and polish the Invicta, Jason and I. Then Friday evening we'd double-date. Sometimes we drove to Boston—a slow, cold crawl up Route One in those days before the Interstate—to stop at Wellesley or Simmons, BC or BU. Radcliff girls were way out of our league.

Other Fridays, we'd end up at nearby Wheaton, Salve Regina in Newport or if things were particularly slow, at the Providence Hospital nursing school. Saturdays we reserved for local Pembroke or RISD dates for the football game and fraternity parties. Sunday afternoons, while Jason memorized the Jupiter Symphony for mid-terms, I went off for long drives with a date. We usually ended with a walk along the beach in Jamestown or Narragansett followed by dinner at an old waterfront bar I liked in Newport.

A 4.5-liter Invicta is a great prop if you want to attract attention. It's also a great way to sort out women. Some took one look and said, "What a funny old car." We dismissed them as foolish girls. And there were some, not as many, it's true, who said, "Wow, is that neat." They became our friends.

My favorite was a Pembroke art major named Marika who thought sneaking into the half-mile Narragansett horse track and drifting the big Invicta sideways around the dirt oval was "Really cool." Her eyes would get all shiny and she'd literally bounce up and down in her excitement as the thick clay pattered off the cycle-type fenders.

A 4.5-liter Invicta is also great for sorting out priorities. Todd no longer had much to do with the car, or us, because he was at Brown to "get an education," taking a dual engineering/business program that was about the hardest thing they offered. He had to become a "grind" just to stay even. Jason The Prodigy did almost no work at all, was still at the top of his class in the music school and had a lucrative job tutoring other music majors.

I abandoned all pretense of being a student, except to drift through an occasional English class. I was a full-time provider for a 4.5-liter Invicta. I drove a truck for the local dry cleaner, washed dishes in the faculty club—I wasn't considered polished enough to wait on tables—sold *Life* magazine over the phone.

Mid-terms showed up the fallacy of this approach. My 1.5 average put me on Academic Probation, which meant I had to get myself up to a 2.0 by the end of the term or find myself drafted to Viet Nam. This was depressing enough, but the Invicta was also showing signs of temperament.

The old Meadows truck engine seemed unbreakable, but Jason and I now spent most of our money and all of our free time fixing little problems with the SU carburetors, the crude electrical system, the tachometer drive, the jury-rigged exhaust system, the creaky old bodywork and especially, the gearshift mechanism.

In their wisdom, the Invicta's designers had mounted the shifter on the right, next to the doorless body side, with a big stainless steel gate to ensure the proper gear. The shift linkage made a right-angle turn above the floor, went across under the driver's legs to the center, made another right-angle turn and headed down to the gearbox. A carpeted cover protected this example of fine British engineering from the driver's feet.

Then there was Jason. He had never driven anything more sporting than his mother's Cadillac. I spent weary afternoons not only trying to teach him how to cope with the peculiarities of a thirty-year-old British sports car that was none too easy to drive even when new, but simply teaching him how to coordinate a clutch and shift lever.

I couldn't tell him no, because the Invicta, after all, was half his. Invariably, however, Jason would go off to visit one of his music students on the other side of town, and call me to come get him in the middle of the night.

Where it connected to the gearbox, the shifter had a particularly vulnerable cotter pin. Jason snapped it with depressing regularity. Then I'd have to lie on my back in a pile of wet leaves and shift the car into gear with my fingers while he waggled the lever. We'd drive home locked in whatever gear I'd been able to find. The next morning, I'd take the thing apart again and make my repairs.

By Christmas vacation, I was under attack on all fronts. The college had notified my parents I was in academic trouble, I had proved spectacularly inept at selling *Life*, I was living on loans cadged from girlfriends and Jason was grudgingly paying all the Invicta's ever-increasing expenses.

The poor old thoroughbred was getting tired of Jason's ham-fisted driving, and it had become impossible to shift into first or reverse. My technology was *not* equal to dismantling the gearbox on a 4.5-liter Invicta. Mostly I worried about what had happened to whatever had broken, and what it was doing to the rest of the gears.

Having no reverse meant we had to plan ahead when parking. To compound the problem, the electrical system had a mysterious short...we couldn't keep a battery charged overnight. Jason was reduced to stealing batteries from other cars...the next morning, they'd be dead as the one I replaced. Luckily, Providence has plenty of hills. I got surprisingly adept at push-starting an Invicta in second, then hopping in over the door as the motor caught.

Christmas vacation required an elaborate plan. All three of us drove to New Haven bundled in Great Uncle Brotherton's coats against the biting cold. Three hours later, when we pulled up to the big house, my feet were so numb it was like driving with concrete blocks instead of shoes. I would *clump* on a pedal I couldn't feel, and the Invicta would do something. Our faces were bright red, our fingers frozen inside pairs of Todd's ski mittens.

His mother was *still* cleaning out undiscovered rooms. We sat in prickly torture while our extremities thawed out. The next morning, she supplied us with another layer of coats and sweaters for the drive to upstate New York. Then Jason and I headed off for Hyde Park, where he dropped me at my parents for a long, long week. They double-teamed me on my grades and the importance of finishing college and how unhappy I would be in the Army. That part I could certainly identify with.

Our plan was that we would tell my parents the Invicta was Jason's and he would tell his parents it was mine. At least that worked. After leaving me, Jason drove home to Long Island, and then came to meet my train from Poughkeepsie on Friday afternoon of Christmas Weekend at Grand Central Station. We planned to drive from New York City to Long Island, spend the weekend with Jason's parents, then stop in New Haven to pick up Todd and yet more antiques on our way to Providence.

I walked out of Grand Central about 4:30, the height of rush hour, carrying my one small suitcase. Jason was right where he said he'd be, drawing an admiring crowd at the corner of Vanderbilt Avenue and 42nd Street. A topless 1933 Invicta in British Racing Green is not exactly what you expect to see in the middle of Manhattan, especially when it's 20 degrees and the forecast is for snow.

I tossed my bag into the rear seat, added an extra topcoat from the supply stored there, and hopped in. Jason slipped the clutch dreadfully to get going, narrowly missing two Checker cabs and a rusted-out '61 Plymouth with no muffler.

"Ahhh, Wad-Wadddya, Waddya," screamed

Jason waving his arms dramatically in imitation of the nearest cab driver who was also leaning on his horn. It was an impressive sight to see a New York driver so thoroughly comfortable in his element. Jason cut off another cab as he went to turn south on Fifth Avenue, only to be waved straight ahead by a policeman. We were now heading West on 42nd Street, directly away from Long Island.

"We-We'll g-g-go around the b-b-block. A-All I have l-l-left is-is t-t-top g-gear."

"Damn. You mean you can't get into second?"

"R-Righ...Exactly."

Of course there was bumper-to-bumper traffic everywhere...it was Friday night rush hour of Christmas Weekend, and everybody in Manhattan was driving out of town. Jason progressed across town in a series of clutch-smoking jolts, a little less smoothly each time as the clutch overheated.

At Ninth Avenue, the policeman waved us into the intersection. The Invicta smoked into the middle of the street, a solid clunk came from the gearbox, and it stopped.

"Oh sh-sh-shit."

The engine was still *whuff, whuffing*, but the Invicta was going nowhere. I jumped out and started pushing. I couldn't budge her. Jason flicked off the ignition, and started pushing on his side of the cowl. Nothing.

By now, the light had changed and we were surrounded by honking, cursing, waving New York City drivers...some trying to go South on Ninth Avenue, some trying to go West on 42nd Street. When they tried to pull around the stalled Invicta, they got stuck in the Eastbound lanes of 42nd

Street, blocking traffic in that direction, too.

The policeman, already red in the face from the cold and exertion, threaded his way to my side of the car. He seemed perplexed to find the steering wheel on the other side.

"Who's da driver heah?"

"I-I-I a-a-am."

"Well, youse gotta move da car."

"It won't roll, Officer. Help us push, maybe we can get it." The three of us pushed with all our might. The Invicta sat as if cemented to the intersection.

"I'm gonna havva calla tow truck. That's gonna cost youse wise guys twenty-five buckos. Plus anudder twenty-five buckos for obstructin' da intasection. That's fifty buckos." He said this with malicious satisfaction and wormed his way towards a phone booth on the corner.

We were in the center of pandemonium, a regular symphony of honking horns and yelling drivers locked in a traffic jam as far as I could see in every direction. There was no way they'd ever get a tow truck within miles of this intersection.

"Fifty dollars! We don't have fifty dollars!"

"H-H-How m-much d-d-d-did w-we p-p-pay f-for t-th-this c-c-car?"

"Fifty dollars."

I looked at Jason. He looked at me. We took off Great Uncle Brotherton's topcoats and laid them gently in the back seat. I picked up my suitcase. I looked around...this was going to take hours. It was just starting to snow, big, wet flakes.

"*And* it's registered to a dead man in New Haven."

There was a Subway entrance on the corner.

Not By Chance

Todd was a kleptomaniac. It's true. My Ivy League college roommate, Chesterton Todd Ward, IV, scion of a proud old New Haven family, would dreamwalk through Warwick Shopper's World and come out with a pocketful of curtain hooks, two tins of shoe polish, three lady's linen handkerchiefs, a crescent wrench, two boxes of 10p nails, a bag of mints, six pairs of plastic earrings and an Elvis Presley photo album.

It wasn't that he wanted this junk; he didn't even know it was spilling from his overcoat pockets. When we got outside, he'd happily divest himself of his hoard and leave it in a pile on the sidewalk. Then he'd go into Gino's Pizza and steal two cold Sicilian slices and a warm Tab.

Unfortunately, my other roommate, the musical prodigy Jason Mildstein, had an older brother who'd also gone to Brown. And Jason had inherited a master key that opened every door on the campus, including the basement storerooms. Pretty soon,

Jason and Todd were making midnight forays. They'd show up at our room, conveniently located on the first floor, with the craziest armloads of mismatched lamps, old books, discarded quilts and ceramic figurines. Half the time, one of the campus guards would be only a corridor behind them, and they'd come tumbling in clutching their booty, panting and laughing over their narrow escape.

For better or worse, we also occupied the largest room on campus, a vast space that was originally intended by the architect to be a student lounge. By Spring of freshman year, our lair had all the cluttered charm of a New England junque shoppe that had been doing business in the same location for a hundred years.

There was a layer of stuff from Todd's late Great Uncle Brotherton's house. There was another layer from Jason's mother, who really did own an antique shoppe on Long Island and sent up all her rejects. There were Todd's various acquisitions, plus the stuff the two of them had wrestled out of basements all over campus.

We finally ran out of storage space when Todd and Jason showed up one night with the complete contents of the Olney House student lounge...a group of hideously color-coordinated orange, green and yellow chairs, two Danish Modern end tables, a matched set of white pole lamps, two neatly framed Views Of The Campus circa 1864...and an eye-wrenching sofa upholstered in electric blue.

Not long after that, the Dean of Students came around to visit us in our cozy nook. Jason had thoughtfully removed all the Brown University labels from the bottoms of the furniture, so Dean Schultz couldn't positively identify the missing lounge furniture as his.

"How long have you boys had this handsome living room set," he asked innocently.

"A-a-a-ll se-se-semes-mester," said Jason, who stammered when he was nervous. "My bubba-bubba-br-brother g-g-gave it t-t-o m-me."

"I see," said Dean Schultz. "I remember Ulysses Mildstein well. Too well. He and I had many hearty little chats like this."

"Oh. Th-that's g-g-reat. M-mom alw-ways s-s-said I'm j-j-just l-like my bubba-bubba...U-U-lys-lyses."

"She did, did she? In that case, I'll tell you and your little friends here the same thing I'd tell him. Next week, over Easter Break, we're going to check every room in this college. I hope for your sake that there are two identical sets of furniture, one in your room and one in the Olney House lounge. Because if there aren't, I can only assume that you have my furniture. I'm told Saigon is very nice, this time of year. *Comprende?*"

And knowing a good exit line when he heard one, Dean Schultz dodged around two aluminum coat racks and squeeged out on his ripple-sole orthopedic shoes, accidentally knocking over an anonymous donor's tableful of souvenirs from the 1964 New York World's Fair.

"Ho-ho-holy sh-sh-it! Wadda-wadda-we go-go-gonna d-d-do?"

"I don't know about you, but I'm calling Harvard to see if my acceptance is still good."

Todd was an engineer, and so he brought the cold light of logic to bear. "What we need," he said, "is a duplicate set of furniture."

"Yeah. R-r-right. Ho-how a-are we g-g-gonna d-d-do t-th-that?"

"Well, this stuff must have come from *some-where*. We'll find out where the college bought it and we'll go there and get another set."

"H-ho-ow? We d-d-don't h-have a-any m-m-money."

"Well, let's see if we can find the furniture first. Then we'll think of something."

"Maybe you can put it in your overcoat pockets and walk out."

Todd ignored me. He had that dreamwalker look, always a dangerous sign. "First we'll need a car to haul the stuff..."

"A c-c-ar? B-but we ha-haven't h-had a c-c-ar since Un-unc-cle Bub-Bub-Brotherton's Invicta d-d-died."

"Exactly. It's about time we had some wheels around here."

We stood in thoughtful silence for a long min-ute.

"I can probably come up with ten dollars," I said hopefully. There was another long silence.

"U-Uh...I-I h-have Un-Unc-Unc...h-h-his c-c-credit c-c-cards."

"What?"

"Jason has Uncle Brotherton's credit cards."

"I heard what he said, I meant 'What' as in 'What the hell are you doing with my dead great uncle's credit cards?'"

"We-well, ya-ya k-kn-know w-when w-we w-were c-c-cleaning out h-his h-house? The c-c-c...they were on t-the t-t-table."

"You mean, you stole my dead uncle's credit cards? Why you dirty, sneaking..."

"Thief? Perhaps poor Jason has been set a bad example. He's an impressionable young lad of only seventeen, you know."

"Se-seventeen a-a-and a h-ha-half."

"Seventeen and a half."

"On the other hand...we *could* rent a car. If I put on a suit and dark glasses, I can pass for over twenty-one. And I know I can forge Uncle's signature. Let's see those credit cards."

The next afternoon about four o'clock, Jason and Todd came piling noisely in just as I was trying to figure out what the little "i" stands for in The Calculus. It looked like any other "i" to me, and had less meaning. I mean, one wants his "i" surrounded by other letters, not just standing there naked.

Actually, I had given up on my textbook, and was reading *Flying* magazine. In it was a story by Richard Bach. His basic argument was that nothing happens by chance, nothing is a coincidence, there is some higher intelligence directing everything that happens to us. If your engine quit on take-off, that was because you were meant to meet this neat old mechanic who lived near the airport and drove a '47 Chevy pickup, not because you had sand clogging your fuel filter.

Maybe God didn't want me to understand The Calculus. Or then, maybe God didn't know what the little "i" stood for, either. Or maybe I wasn't meant to pass Math 101, which was looking more and more like a possibility. I was sure God had never reckoned on the synergistic effect of putting Jason and Todd together in the same dorm room.

"Todd, you're the math wiz, what the hell does the little "i" *mean*?"

Todd ignored me. Jason grabbed my arm and dragged me off the couch.

"Co-come s-s-see wh-what Uncle B-Brotherton rented f-for us!"

Their rent-a-car was parked in front of the dorm with an admiring crowd of freshman standing around it. They even had the hood propped up.

"What the...you've gotta be kidding! They let you have a *Shelby Mustang*? On Uncle Brotherton's credit card?"

"Yeah," said Todd shyly. "But I had to lie and tell the girl I was twenty-five. She was pretty cute, actually. And Uncle Brotherton had to join the Hertz Sports Car Club. See, here's his card."

I circled warily. Sure as hell, parked at the curb was a shiny black Mustang fastback with gold stripes down the middle, five-spoke Cragar wheels and "G.T.350H" decals on the rocker panels. It was every schoolboy's dream, just sitting there. Why, it even had racing seat belts, a fake wood steering wheel and *hood pins*. And a decal under the radio that read "This vehicle is equipped with competition brakes. Heavier than normal brake pedal pressure may be required." *Competition brakes*. I thought I'd faint.

"Can I drive it?"

"N-n-no, m-m-me!"

"You, you don't even have a driver's license."

"I d-do, to-too. I just c-c-can't d-d-drive at n-night."

"We can *all* drive. But my Great Uncle Brotherton rented it. So *I* get to drive first."

I pushed Jason into the cramped back seat and

scrambled into the passenger seat. Aware of the dozens of eyes watching him, Todd walked slowly around the Mustang, closed and pinned the hood, opened the door, slipped behind the wheel, settled himself in the seat, clicked the competition seat belts, checked the mirrors. Everyone waited.

Then *braam, braam, BRAAM*, the Shelby exhaust bounced around the Quad. We all listened, lips parted in ecstacy. Todd shifted the automatic into *D* and stuck his foot into the firewall. We burned rubber all the way to Waterman Street.

I looked back, and the crowd of kids was a mass of eyeballs staring enviously after us. They were almost obscured in a cloud of blue tire smoke. Todd narrowly missed a Valiant pulling into our block, screeched mostly sideways around the corner and rocketed down the hill towards the center of Providence. We were going furniture shopping.

Thursday went by. Friday went by. We sucked up two tanks of Sunoco 260 visiting every furniture store, every department store, every place that had so much as a lamp or a barstool within 20 miles of Providence. Little stores, big stores. Stores with condescending salesmen under bad haircuts and stores with helpful little old ladies. Even one with a snarling Doberman under a Formica desk.

Nothing. Nobody had anything that resembled our borrowed lounge furniture. And time was running out. Easter Break started Monday, and we all had to leave Sunday for home or risk the dread Parental Inquisition. Our last chance was Saturday. If we couldn't duplicate that ridiculous living room set by Saturday night, we'd be talking to our draft boards within weeks and shouldering M16s before the Fourth of July. The situation was desperate.

We searched further afield on Saturday, blasting up and down the interstate at 90 mph to Warwick, East Providence, Fall River. Nothing. And then, like we were characters in a bad B-movie, just as we were at our lowest point, Todd took the wrong exit off I-95 and dumped us into a poor part of town we'd never seen before, out beyond Atwells Avenue. We wandered around looking for the Interstate, and instead we found what looked like an old neighborhood shopping area, gone to seed. The Shelby attracted all sorts of attention, but we were used to that by now.

"H-hey. St-st-stop. Th-the-there."

Jason was right. It was a furniture store that couldn't have changed much since 1929. The facade was yellow brick, there was yellow translucent plastic over the windows to keep the sun from fading the furniture and hand-lettered signs that screamed "NO MONEY DOWN" and "FINAL CLEARANCE, EVERYTHING MUST GO."

Todd parked the Shelby right in front of the doors, and we tumbled in. A crowd of guys in black leather jackets had formed around our car before the store doors had even stopped swinging. When I looked back over my shoulder, they were opening the Shelby's hood. I touched Todd on the shoulder and pointed, but he just kept staring towards the back corner of the store. I followed his gaze until my eyes were assaulted by a familiar electric blue couch and three yellow, green and orange chairs.

"Momma, I'm home," said Todd in a barely audible whisper.

Maybe Richard Bach knew something I didn't.

"Hello, boys. My name is Murphy. Pat Murphy. Can I help you?"

Mr. Murphy was wearing a decent tweed blazer, red and white rep tie and Bass Weejuns. It was a get-up much more appropriate to an English Lit. graduate seminar than a dusty furniture store on the wrong side of town.

"We-we n-n-need th-th..." Jason's voice tapered off, overcome by the emotion of the moment. Mr. Murphy retained his alert and interested look.

"What he means," said Todd, "is that we'd like to buy, I mean to borrow, I mean..."

"Are you boys students at Brown, by any chance?"

"Yes sir. We're freshman. And we have this problem."

"Well, perhaps I can help. I'm a Brown man myself, class of '38. My brother is in the office. He's class of '36."

That explained the tweeds, but what the hell were they doing here? Richard Bach would say they'd been sent to help us out. So I figured the best tactic was to tell Mr. Murphy the truth. Obviously, there was some great plan at work, here. A plan I knew nothing about. I wondered when the aircraft mechanic with the '47 Chevy pickup would appear.

"Well, Mr. Murphy, it's like this. We were playing a harmless student prank, got ourselves in trouble with Dean Schultz, and only you can help us out."

"College Pranks! I love 'em." Mr. Murphy's polite smile turned up another 100 watts to incandescent.

"Why one time, my brother Ed and I took

Nobby Hortwhistle's Model A and parked it in Sayles Hall. You know Sayles Hall? It was a bitch getting it up those stairs. And another time, we filled Dean Carberry's closet with water with a little hose through the keyhole. When he opened the door...

"Here's Ed now." Ed was a carbon copy of his brother, right down to the old school tie and the shiny red nose.

"These boys were just going to tell us how we can help them with a prank up at the college."

I looked at Jason, who looked at Todd, who looked at me. Were these guys for real, or what?

"Well, Mr. Murphy, like I say, we took all the furniture from Olney House lounge—you know Olney House?—and we put it in a friend's room. And Dean Schultz says he's going to throw our friend out of Brown for stealing the furniture unless there are two sets, one in his room and one in the lounge, by tomorrow. So we were wondering, like, a...could we borrow that blue sofa and those three chairs and the pole lamps? And the end tables? Just for a week..."

I held my breath. Pat Murphy looked at Ed. Ed Murphy looked at Pat. They both smiled incandescent smiles. "Do you have your Brown ID cards? If we could write the numbers down, I don't see why you shouldn't borrow that furniture. Just bring it back when you're done."

"Gee, thanks Mr. Murphy."

"That's okay. That's okay. It's been sitting there for years. Somebody up at Brown ordered two sets like that, we delivered one, they cancelled the second one. Never could understand why."

"Gee, thanks Mr. Murphy."

"Oh, our pleasure. Always glad to help a fellow student out of a jam. You know, you boys are lucky to find us. There were only two sets of furniture like that in the whole world. It was a custom order."

We were all smiling like light bulbs at our mutual good fortune when the unmistakable sound of a Shelby Mustang starting up filled the showroom. *Braam, Braam, BRAAM*.

"Was that you boys in the hot Mustang? Well, I think my son Patrick just borrowed it for a moment. It amuses him to try and start cars without the key."

"What! But Mr. Murphy, that's car theft," said Todd pulling himself up on his toes in righteous indignation. "He stole my car. Er, my uncle's car..."

"Oh, don't worry. Patrick's not all there, sometimes, but he's a very good driver. Wins drag races on Atwells Avenue all the time, they tell me."

"What?"

"Yep. That's probably where he's heading right now."

"This is crazy!" I went running towards the door. I swung it open with all my might, and the girl who had just grabbed the handle from the outside was swept off her feet. I had a momentary impression of a cloud of vivid red hair, freckles, blue sunglasses and somebody socking me in the stomach with what felt like a bowling ball. We went down in a heap on the floor, with me spread-eagled beneath her.

"Aaargh," she screamed in my ear, and then I felt something rake across my cheek. It stung like hell. She was just raising her hand to scratch me again when I got a scissor hold around her legs, grabbed her wrists and flipped her over on her back on the floor. I hadn't been on the high school wrestling team for nothing.

"Let me go, you clumsy brute...Oh. I might have known. You're from Brown. Christ, you're in my art class."

It's true. The disheveled redhead I helped from the floor was a Pembroke coed named Debrah, and we sat at opposite sides of the studio in Professor Koren's Principles of Composition 101. What a Pembroker was doing on the wrong side of town, in a rundown furniture store, it didn't occur to me to ask. I suppose she was wondering the same thing about me.

Debrah was a theatre major, an actress with an incredibly pretty and mobile face that constantly moved from one expression to another as though she were practicing for an audition..."Give me happy, Honey. Good. Now give me sad. Give me grief, give me mixed emotions...your husband's been killed, but now you can marry your boyfriend. Good. Great. Come back tomorrow, I might have something."

She was also addicted to The Dramatic Gesture, tossing her wonderful crimson mane back from her face with a practiced flip of an arched wrist and then doing this thing of playing the harp in her hair, like a *Vogue* model. She also roiled her legs around in her miniskirt a lot—she had great legs—showing lots of thigh. And she smoked cigarettes in that sexy way Carol Lombard smoked in old movies, as an elegant substitute for intercourse.

Debrah was what my mother would have labelled with a sniff, *theatrical*. I found her fascinating, and had spent long hours of art class memorizing and trying to draw her dozens of moods. She would never even smile in my direction, and when she found me staring at her legs, she'd snap her knees together and swivel away from me.

"I'm sorry, it's just that somebody stole our car and I was running to try and stop him."

Her face softened slightly, from iceberg to deep freeze. Now she was Grace Kelly in *To Catch A Thief*. "Oh, was that your Shelby I saw Patrick driving? Don't worry. I know where he's going. Come on."

She grabbed my hand, dragged me outside and sort of flung me into the passenger seat of a top-down turquoise Mustang convertible with mag wheels. It had a white Pony interior, some extra gauges hung under the radio and a tachometer on top of the dash.

"Hang on," she said dramatically, and slewed off in hot pursuit. She was pretty good, I'll say that for her. She angled across town, block by block. *Gas-brake-turn. Gas-brake-turn. Gas-brake-turn.* She could keep the tires screeching nearly all the time in one direction or another.

I'd stared at her so much in Art 101, I knew most of her expressions. Driving fast, she was biting her lower lip and leaning eagerly forward. This was her Look of Intense Concentration, commonly used to impress Professor Koren with how much she hung on his every word.

It was interesting to see it wasn't *all* an act. She really did bite her lip when she was concentrating on something. Her incredible mass of red hair swirled around her head in the wind, and every once in a while she'd fling it out of her eyes with that gesture I knew so well.

"This Mustang is pretty quick." I was plastered against the door, holding on to the dashboard for support.

"Yeah," she yelled above the wind and exhaust noise. "My old boyfriend built the engine for it...350 hp on the dyno. Shelby suspension, Goodyear Blue Streaks, the whole bit. Great car, even if he turned out to be a real drip after I went to college."

"What are you doing out here, anyway? Shopping for furniture?"

"You are a jerk! That's my father's store. We live behind it, on the next block." She glanced at me demurely, Vivien Leigh's Scarlett O'Hara looking up at Rhett Butler...in the middle of a screeching four-wheel drift. "I'm a day student. A townie. A street meat."

"I could swear his name was Mr. Murphy. The man who owns the store. Your father."

"Did you ever hear of an actress named Debbie Murphy? Ugh."

"So you made up Debrah D'Arcy-D'Urbanville?"

"Is there anything wrong with that?"

"Uh, no...uh, it's a great name. For an actress. Very memorable."

"Yeah. Well. My friends call me 3-D."

And with that, she expertly slid the Mustang sideways onto Atwells Avenue, cutting off some old guy in a '47 Chevy pickup, and braked to a stop just inches from Todd's Shelby. The same group of black leather jackets surrounded the car, and the hood was up. Next to the Shelby was a red Plymouth Belvedere with 426 emblems. And next to that was a black 442 Oldsmobile. In front was a dark blue big block Sting Ray with side pipes.

The biggest, meanest-looking black leather jacket hunched over to us. He reached into the car, picked up Debrah under both arms, the way a gorilla would steal a baby, lifted her over the door and kissed her full on the lips.

"Hi Debbie."

She gave him the same cheekful of nails I'd already gotten. "Rico, goddamnit, put me down."

"Whatsa matter, Baby, on the rag?" He stood her on her feet and looked at me. "Hey, you get yours da same way?" He peered suspiciously at the red welts and the dried blood on my cheek.

"No, no," I mumbled. "Ran into a door."

"Yeah. Right."

"He wants his car back," explained Debbie. "That's his Shelby."

"It's Irving Hertz's Shelby," corrected Rico. "But he's welcome to it. Piece a crap got beat three outa three runs by Bobby's Vette. It won't get out of its own way. We was just checkin' da timing."

"You probably don't know how to drive it. Let me try."

"Hey guys, Debbie here wants ta run da Shelby against Bobby's Vette."

I expected this would get a big guffaw from Da Guys, but *au contraire*. They solemnly buckled her into the Shelby, got the mysterious Bobby and his Sting Ray lined up next to her and heading up Atwells Avenue—this entailed much waving of arms and countermanding of directions—and then stopped traffic for three blocks ahead by the simple expedient of standing in the cross streets and threatening any driver who tried to pull onto the track.

It was insane. Six o'clock on Saturday night,

one of the main arteries in Providence, and these folks were running a full scale street race complete with side bets. The odds seemed to be 10 to 3 for Bobby, 8 to 2 against Debbie. I figured I had Richard Bach on my side. I put down my last $10 on Debbie in the Shelby. I could always borrow something from Jason for train fare home tomorrow, and once there, my Dad was usually good for a fifty.

Of course she won and I promptly collected $40. Debbie pulled a hole shot on the Corvette that left him a length behind, then edged over towards his lane just enough that he wasn't sure he could get by without wrecking his Sting Ray against the parked cars. So he stayed right on her bumper. She slowed to let him by after the finish line, flipped him the finger along with her best Marilyn Monroe smile, then spun the Shelby around in an expert J-turn. She was back to the start before Bobby had even gotten turned around.

She squeaked to a stop next to the Mustang. "The cops will be here any second. Follow me."

She went blasting off in the Shelby, with me half-a-block behind in her convertible. I could hear sirens somewhere behind us. She led me back to the store through the same confusing tangle of streets, blasting along as fast as she could go. Her convertible was just as fast, and I could stay with her if I worked at it. We finished up in a cloud of tire smoke, nose-to-tail in front of "EVERYTHING MUST GO."

"Wh-where th-the h-h-hell h-h-have yy-you b-been?"

"Getting back the Shelby."

"Well, Mr. Murphy had to lock up. He lent us the furniture, some pads and ropes. What a guy."

"Yeah. His daughter's pretty nice, too."

Debbie gave me Maureen O'Hara doing Mixed Emotions to John Wayne, mad but pleased. Then she helped us rope the chairs on top of the Shelby. With some squeezing, the tables fit in the back seat.

"If you want to wait here, Jason and I can bring this up to school and come right back."

"You guys can put the rest in my convertible. You'll never get that couch in a Shelby, anyway."

And so we balanced that awful blue couch across the back of Debbie's Mustang, tied it down, then stuck the pole lamps behind the bucket seats.

"Why do you guys want this junk, anyway?"

"It's a long story, which I'll be happy to tell you on the way."

"Ummph."

Since I still had the key to her car in my hand, I hopped into the driver's seat. She glared at me for a long minute, then climbed into the passenger seat.

"You're the navigator. We don't know how we got here, or how to get back. We don't even know where we are."

Debbie directed me across town, kneeling on the seat and holding onto the couch with one hand. The wind blew her hair into a tangle, but I caught her looking at me a couple of times. She was doing Puzzled, I think. Or maybe Unsure.

I pulled quietly up near our dorm and parked in the shadows. We didn't really need anybody watching us move two sets of furniture around, especially the campus guards or Dean Schultz. Happily, almost everybody had either already gone home for Easter Break, or was out for Saturday night.

While Debbie stayed with the cars, Jason, Todd and I wrestled the famous Olney House furniture out of our room, across The Quad and back into its lounge where it could be an eyesore for yet another generation of Brown freshmen.

Then we unloaded the cars and sneaked Mr. Murphy's furniture into our room. It looked precisely the same as the other set.

"I w-w-wish I c-c-could s-see the l-l-look on D-Dean S-S-Schultz's-s f-face w-when he s-s-sees t-th-this!"

"Me too. But just as long as I don't see Saigon in the Summer, I'll be happy."

"I bet he never thought we could do it. He's gonna just shit."

When I got back out to the curb, the blue Sting Ray was sitting in the middle of the street, idling, and Debbie was obviously arguing with a dark haired guy in a black leather jacket. She had bright red spots on each cheek. She turned towards me, smiled for effect, then took my hand and kissed me quickly on the cheek with the scratches. It hurt like hell, frankly. She held me close, one arm wrapped around mine.

"I'd like you to meet my *ex*-boyfriend, Bobby. He was just leaving." Now she was Ingrid Bergman in *Casablanca*.

Bobby clenched and unclenched his fists and got very red in the face.

"Are you the one who built the engine in Debbie's Mustang? It's really strong."

He had a nice smile. "Thanks. I put a lot of work into that motor. Take care of it for me."

Bobby laid down two streaks of rubber right

over the ones Todd had put down a couple of days before. Was that only two days ago? It seemed like a lifetime.

"W-w-what's h-h-happening?"

"Yeah. Who the hell was that greaser in the Corvette? We're starving. Want to get something to eat?"

"Uh, Debbie and I are going out to dinner at this place she knows across town."

"We are?"

"Yes. We are." I still had her hand. I steered her into the passenger seat of the Mustang, carefully shut and locked the door and hopped behind the wheel. *Braam, Braam, BRAAM.* I shifted the console automatic. Then I grabbed Debbie's hand and held it.

"I have to tell her about a guy named Richard Bach. He says nothing ever happens by chance."

"Bullshit. There is a Random Theory, you know, that says everything in the universe happens randomly. You study it in Quantum Physics."

"Who's the professor?"

"Dean Schultz."

"It figures. Tell him from me, he's wrong. Dead wrong."

One Sunday In July

The summer of 1966 fell between my Sophomore and Junior years at Brown University. I was living with my parents in upstate New York, and working two jobs. From midnight until 8:00 am, I ran a computer in IBM's R&D lab in Kingston, testing the very first 360/90 equipped with a CRT and a light pen on a cable.

When my shift ended, I'd run out to the parking lot, and hop into my 1952 MG TD. It was red, with black seats and gray carpets that my mother had cut from her old living room rug. The way you could tell was by the flower patterns shaved into the pile. The shift knob was the wooden cap off a bottle of English Leather, and I had replaced the bumpers with nerf bars from the Strauss store in Poughkeepsie.

Like Clark Kent, I'd change out of my suit and tie—short hair, blue suits and white shirts only, please, at IBM in the Sixties—and into my bathing suit. Try that sometime, sitting in an MG TD. Then I'd drive twenty miles over delicious back country roads to the town swimming pool in Hyde Park. I didn't own side-curtains for the TD, and I never bothered to put the top up.

My first swimming class started at 9:00 am, Intermediate Swimming for eight and nine year olds. I taught swimming till noon, ate lunch with the other lifeguards in the shade of a huge old maple on the grounds of the former estate, and then played lifeguard from one till five. Then I'd rush home and fall into a catatonic stupor for five hours, until my mother would call me at 10:00 pm to eat breakfast before commuting to work at midnight.

That whole summer passed with a kind of brilliant clarity induced by lack of sleep, lack of food and eight hours a day in the sun. I saw everything as though from a great distance, but at the same time, in great detail. I would scan the pool looking for signs of trouble, and find myself focusing on the pattern of sun and shadow on the bottom. I'd be running a computer test program at 3:00 am in a lab by myself, and wake up five hours later when the next shift came in and kicked my chair over backwards, laughing as I thrashed around on the floor trying to get my footing in the coils of computer cable.

The weirdest days were Saturdays. I'd get off work, and the older guys I worked with would drag me to the local bar, which opened at 9:00 am. You ever been in a bar at 9:00 am? Patsy Kline would be singing on the jukebox. There were always three or four middle-age men reading the sports pages, two more working over the racing form and a washed-out blonde reading *True Confessions*.

Most of them had a shot of bourbon and a beer on the counter, and like my friends, were just settling in till closing time, seventeen hours in the future. Danny the bartender and I drank coffee and talked about Formula One racing. He was a great Jack Brabham fan, while I had rowed on the high school crew which made me partial to fellow oarsman Graham Hill. Danny rode a Honda 305 Super Hawk, and was always challenging me to race him. I never did, because I knew he'd win and then I'd never hear the end of it.

After an hour or so, I'd bail out against a wave of jeers about college boys who didn't know how to have a good time. I'd drive home the long way, chasing down all the back roads I could find in rural Dutchess County, totally empty at that hour except perhaps for a red-faced farmer on a John Deere, pulling a hay wagon. Sliding around in the gravel on skinny little tires, windshield folded down if Danny had gotten me especially riled up, was a lot more fun than anything those bar flies could invent to wile away the hours.

My new girlfriend Jean, who went to Rhode Island School of Design, was spending the summer working for a family who had a house on the ocean in Narragansett. They had fourteen-year-old twins, and Jean—all of nineteen—was their combination nanny/chauffeur. Mostly, it meant she spent her days at the posh Narragansett Beach Club, and her evenings driving the twins for pizza or to rock concerts—they even went to Boston to see the Beatles on tour.

She finally received permission for me to come visit for a weekend. So one Saturday morning near the end of July, instead of heading towards Delaney's Fiesta Grill and then racing aimlessly around,

I pointed the TD up Route 44 and pottered along to Hartford, and then Route 6 over to Providence, then Route 2 to Narragansett...in those days, all narrow rural roads, almost deserted even on a summer Saturday.

The TD was perfect for those lightly-trafficked two-lanes. I could cruise along at 65, and drift around the sweeping corners without lifting...all arms and elbows from the tight seating position. Compared to modern sports cars, my old MG was pretty thin gruel, but it also was never serious. It was always a happy car that made you smile, and made other people smile with you.

I was bronze from the sun, thin from not eating and fit from swimming every day. Driving to work in my bathing suit, I'd gotten into the vain-glorious habit of tooling around with my shirt off in the top-down TD. I baked bare and lightheaded in the sun all the way to Narragansett, and it had turned into a brutally hot evening by the time I rolled up to the stone gateposts that marked the end of the driveway where Jean was staying.

There was a long winding drive through acres of lawn, a couple of Richardsonian stone and shingle carriage houses converted into summer cottages and then, right on the cliffs, a gigantic stone mansion from the 1880s, complete with turrets, tower and an arched *porte cochere*. Beyond it, I could see Atlantic surf pounding on a jumble of rocks, each the size of a Volkswagen.

I parked the tired but self-satisfied TD between an immaculate, navy blue Mercedes 300SEL and a salt-encrusted Jeep Wagoneer. Just as I finished pulling my shirt over my head, the varnished oak front door swung open and Jean tackled me from behind. She was so delicate and so pretty...no taller than my shoulder, fabulous tan summer legs, big brown eyes and short dark hair with a wide blonde streak from the sun. She was wearing sandals, her favorite purple mini-dress and big tortoise-shell hoop earrings from an antique shop on Benefit Street. I hugged her so hard I was afraid I'd break a rib, and we kissed until we both ran out of air.

Hand-in-hand like children in a forest, she walked me through the house. There was an immense hall, a formal dining room, a sunroom, a living room lined with books and chintz-covered antiques...all eerily unoccupied. Jean led me over to a door hidden in one corner of the living room. I opened it, and stepped into the billiard room. At the near end was a Victorian billiard table covered in green baize, with real Tiffany lamps hanging over it for illumination. Behind it was rack full of billiard cues and three dark red leather armchairs.

At the far end of the oak-lined room, two men in sweat-drenched T-shirts and blue jeans were bending over the engine compartment of a blue and white Mustang GT-350R racing car. Behind them was a dark blue open-wheel Formula car on orange jackstands. My surprise couldn't have been more complete...it was like opening a door in London in 1880 and stepping into the paddock at Laguna Seca. For a minute, I thought I was hallucinating from fatigue and sunstroke. Jean laughed in delight at my confusion. The two grease-stained men looked up when they heard her laugh.

It turned out that the younger, heavier one was Myron Baldridge, the graying, skinny one was his imported British mechanic, Tony Something. Myron's mother and her new husband owned the house, and since he didn't have anywhere else to work, they'd let Myron knock a hole through the billiard room wall, install a garage door and set up a race shop.

I guess it made sense in a crazy sort of way, though in those days Jean and I had a nice apartment in Providence—with garage—that we rented for $20 a month. Surely Myron could have rented a shop anywhere in Rhode Island for less than it cost to knock out a wall of the house—it was built of cobblestone—and install a door.

The blue open-wheeler was a Lotus 20B Formula car, a couple of years old, with its 1498cc Ford engine replaced by a 1600cc Alfa-Romeo four-cylinder from a Conrero-prepared GTZ that some friend of Myron's had crashed. The result was an ill-handling, unreliable racer for Formula B, a class that almost nobody else contested and in which Myron was therefore a contender.

The GT-350 was something else, completely. Tasco Ford in Providence was the biggest Shelby dealer on the East Coast, and Myron had paid them full list for a factory-prepared Shelby Mustang race car for B-Production. It had every R-type option, a stripped interior, five-spoke American Racing magnesium wheels and more horsepower than anything else in Rhode Island. I think Myron might have driven it once or twice, but very early on he had realized it was not a car for a wealthy enthusiast, but a deadly-serious weapon for a professional racing driver.

That professional was Mark Donohue. I knew

a little bit about Mark, because he'd graduated from Brown in 1959, and become something of a school legend. Myron Baldridge Racing—which consisted of Myron and Tony Something—had sponsored Mark the year before, when he got the SCCA's Kimberly Cup by winning both Formula B with the Lotus and B-Production with the Shelby. I had read about it in a couple of magazine articles.

In 1966, Myron was racing the repowered Lotus, and Mark was running the Mustang when he had time, in between driving in his first season for Roger Penske. He and Penske had a Chevrolet-powered Lola for the new Can-Am series, and it was already obvious to everyone—except perhaps to Myron—that Mark Donohue was about to outgrow Myron Baldridge Racing.

It turned out that the reason Myron and Tony were working late on a Saturday night was because there was a race at Thompson, Connecticut the next afternoon, and Mark was meeting them there. We could come if we wanted. I had spent summer weekends at Lime Rock for years—my father was a mechanical engineer at IBM, and most of the guys who worked for him seemed to spend all their spare time building race cars and were always looking for gofers. But Jean had never been to a car race of any kind, and I had never been to Thompson. And certainly not as guests of Myron Baldridge Racing.

That night we had dinner with Jean's employers, Mr. and Mrs. Folsom. Their conversation tended towards the stock market, members of the Brown and RISD Boards of Trustees we'd never heard of and the disgraceful behavior of young people at the Narragansett Beach Club this year. The twins had been packed off to friends for the evening, while Myron and Tony skipped dinner to continue working on the Mustang.

We knew it was back together when the sudden and unmistakable boom of a racing V-8 set the crystal vibrating on the dining table during dessert. After dinner, Mr. Folsom led me into the chintz living room and quizzed me like a prospective son-in-law while his wife rested and Jean cleaned up. It was a curious arrangement...Jean fit somewhere between friend of the family, Cinderella and hired help. Compared to IBM, though, it sure seemed like a nice place to work. When we finally went up to bed, Myron and Tony were still hard at work in the billiard room, having closed the hood on the Mustang and switched to the disemboweled Lotus.

The family used the first and second floors. I had been given one of the guest rooms in a tower on the third floor; morning revealed a completely round room, furnished in antique white wicker, with dramatic views of dawn breaking over the ocean.

At breakfast with the family, the twins turned out to be a gorgeous pair of blondes—one male, one female—much too sophisticated to talk to someone like me or to be bothered to ride all the way to Connecticut on a hot day to watch their stepbrother race. They soon wandered off to the beach, which was fine with me. I wanted to be alone with Jean, anyway.

Myron and Tony Something had rigged a set of ramps on the back of a Chevy pickup, and by removing its nose cone, the Lotus could be squeezed up there. The Shelby rode behind on an open trailer. They gave us quick directions and roared off to make practice. Jean and I drove more slowly, enjoying the morning, the sun, the winding roads and each other. It was noon before we found our way to Thompson, in upstate Connecticut.

Thompson Raceway was even less imposing than Lime Rock. There were some some dusty parking lots filled with tow rigs, mostly American station wagons with open trailers. There were unpainted wooden barriers around the pits, and the course used half of a small paved oval as a banked "carrousel" like the Nurburgring. On Wednesday and Friday nights, they raced Modified Stocks on the oval, and all the signs on the wooden fences were from local speed shops and garages. It was as if road racing and foreign cars didn't exist.

After the banked oval, the road course disappeared over a hill, wandered around a bit through some esses cut into the woods and came back down a short straight to start another lap. We pulled the MG nearly to the pit wall, next to the pickup and trailer. Nobody tried to stop us.

Myron and Tony had the Lotus apart again, looking for a high-rpm miss. Mark still hadn't shown up. He'd raced somewhere else on Saturday, and was doing one of those manic all-nighters to get to Thompson in time for the race. Having missed qualifying, he'd have to start at the back, but that was deemed Not a Problem by Myron and Tony. The way they talked, it didn't matter if Mark started in the next county, he'd still win in a walk.

Jean and I sat behind the pit wall in folding chairs rescued from somewhere inside the pickup bed, and only slightly flecked with greasy dirt. It was achingly hot and humid, and we sat as still as possible, to keep cool. The only spectators were family and friends of the racers, and everybody else seemed to know each other. A fine coating of dust settled over everything, including us, our Cokes and our hot-dogs before we could eat them.

The first race was a mixed bag of H-Production Bugeye Sprites, Fiat-Abarth sedans and small sports/racers. E and F-Production was mostly MGAs and Porsche Speedsters, along with a couple of Turners and Elva Couriers. Then there were some medium-size Lotus and Lola sports/racers in their own classes. C and D-Production consisted of Triumph TR-4s, Morgans and Austin-Healeys.

Then there were even larger sports/racers, most of them home-built around American V-8s. There was a modified C-Jag, and a Buick-engined XK-140 with a handmade fiberglass body that had been built years ago by an engineer named Ray Griffith, who worked with my father. I had been his pit crew, and I always thought the car looked like a burnt baked potato, with its ripply body sprayed in dark gray primer. Now it had a new owner, who had painted it an excrutiating yellow, but it still didn't run worth a damn.

Myron started on the pole for the Open-Wheeler race, but progressed steadily towards the back as the misfire got worse and worse. He was obviously getting angrier and angrier, throwing the car around in great time-wasting slides. Tony kept his head down, muttering. Finally, the engine quit out on the course, and Myron coasted into the pits. He threw himself out of the car, threw his helmet on the ground and stalked off. Not a car owner I'd want to work for, I decided.

As if by magic, Mark was suddenly there. I was half-asleep from the sun and fatigue, and it seemed as though he had sprung up through the ground, wearing his driving suit. The last race group was already assembling on the grid, and Jean and I helped Tony push the Mustang into the very back. There were some elderly Corvettes, some later Sting Rays, a brace of XKEs, a couple of Porsche 911s and a single Shelby Cobra driven by somebody Mark seemed to know, and with whom he chatted while they waited on the grid.

At the five minute signal, he ambled over and let Tony belt him into the Mustang. He was taller and thinner than you'd expect, with a kind of lanky, raw-boned charm. His crew cut was so short you could see his scalp, and he had that remote, far-seeing stare that I'd come to recognize as the sign of an engineer. It wasn't that they ignored you, it was that they existed in a separate world, devoid of interpersonal relationships. My father always seemed like he was reading something in the air about a foot over your head, and Mark had that same detached manner.

He pulled his helmet on, and reached out the window to shake hands with Tony and I. He looked just like the picture in the Sunoco ads; his open-face helmet was always kind of perched on the back of his head, with his fat baby cheeks and wide grin dwarfing his face. He was young, happy and overwhelming confident...someone doing what he wanted to be doing, and who knew he could do it very, very well.

The race was anticlimatic. The pack thundered off in a crescendo of basso profundo V-8s, and Mark simply motored around them until he was at the front rather than the back. By the end, he had lapped most of the field, and you could see his grin as he passed the pits every lap. Myron appeared in time to take a victory lap in the passenger seat, holding the checkered flag out the window. When Mark came in, he was still smiling, though now sweat was literally running off him and his face was glowing red.

Jean got him something to drink and Tony gave him a wet towel to wash his face, while Myron fussed with the Mustang, looking for damage that wasn't there. Mark shook hands all around again with that detached manner, then hitched a ride with friends and was gone to the Hartford airport to catch a plane for Toronto, where he was testing tomorrow for Penske at Mosport. He couldn't have been at Thompson more than an hour.

Jean and I motored off soon after, leaving Tony and Myron to load up the two cars and trailer home. We parked at a roadside rest area in Connecticut where there was a stream, and waded in, clothes and all, to splash around for ten minutes. That got rid of most of the sweat-caked dust, and we were air-dry again after a couple of miles in the TD. We had a favorite German restaurant on Route 6, outside Providence, and we stopped there on our way to Narragansett for sauerbrauten, spaetzel and beer.

I always liked driving the TD best at night...the dim glow of the instruments, the little Lucas running lights on the fenders, the patterns of on-coming traffic, the constantly-changing roof of the constellations. Damp night smells came off the fields, mixed with the acrid scent of cow barns and the sweet aroma of newly-cut hay. As we got near the coast, the wonderful mixed smells that came off the ocean seemed almost electric in the air. Holding hands, Jean and I cruised slowly home and quietly climbed the stairs to the big round room in the tower.

Monday morning, we were awakened by the sound of the Mustang being driven into the billiard room. By the time we ate breakfast and wandered into the shop, Tony had the heads off and was making neat piles of parts along one wall. Myron had already gone to Providence for Alfa ignition parts. Jean took the twins to the beach club in the Wagoneer, and I followed in the TD.

I stayed for lunch, and then started the long drive home, into the sun, so I could be at work again by midnight. I'd taken Monday off from the pool, and I'd have to make that up by working evenings for adult swimming the rest of the week. That meant no sleep at all, except what I could steal at IBM by feeding in a long test program that would run by itself for hours, while I napped with my head on the console.

The next Saturday morning, I stopped by Delaney's after work to talk with Danny. I told him about my weekend, and meeting Mark Donohue and Myron Baldridge. He acted like he believed me, but I don't think he did. I hadn't even thought of getting Mark's autograph; I hadn't even bought a program at Thompson. That Saturday morning, I pushed especially hard in the TD, pretending I was racing and wondering what it was really like out there. Then I went home and slept for twenty-four hours.

I had a dream in which I raced against Mark Donohue. Jean was in the Shelby with him, and he would zoom ahead, and then wait around the corners for me to show up in my MG. They would both laugh at me, and zoom away again. It went on and on, racing through corner after corner, down dark tunnels lined with bright green trees. I could never catch up.

The Night They Drove the Old 'Vette Down

I remember the night Mark Silvers bought his Corvette. We were all sitting around the stove in Clarence Ripley's garage, holding our regular, weekly lie-swapping session after washing and polishing everything in sight. We weren't organized enough to have a club or anything like that, but all the regulars were there. The most puissant machine in the yard was Dwayne Moore's Healey Hundred, which should tell you something. My red MG TD was the group weakling, but I consoled myself with the myth that I made up in charm what I lacked in horsepower.

Clarence was a middle-aged mechanic, bald as an egg, with fat pink cheeks and a lopsided grin anchored at the low end to a dead White Owl. He was sarcastic and vulgar, specializing in remarks to the effect that fine cars were wasted on young fools like us, etc. etc. ad nauseum. If you could stand the insults, though, he was the only one this side of Boston willing to try and fix a car the way we brought them in.

I mean, you could hardly tell unless you knew where to look that I'd shaved the top four inches off my MG trying to beat the rapidly descending mock-Gothic main gate of the local girls' college, right at closing time. I've still got a scar down the top of my head to remind me, with sloppy stitches courtesy of the South Attleboro emergency squad. In Clarence's hands the MG came out better than my scalp.

The Ripley Garage was in a prime location. Past the door of the converted farmhouse went State Road 29, a mostly deserted two-lane highway bordered with picturesque New England farms and fir trees that wound its way up and down about five miles into town, with a wicked set of Esses at the end that invariably decided who was going to buy the first round at the Attleboro Tavern. This was our medium-speed test track.

Across the street from Clarence's was a formidable swamp traversed by a pot-holed gravel road that wandered wickedly off into the hills. It took a demon to average thirty over Old Swamp Road, and one little mistake meant a slimy swim. Further on, up in the hills, it ran along next to a streambed for a while, crossed over a one-lane bridge above a waterfall and eventually ended up in Harvey Foreman's Back Forty with a rusted harrow and the remains of a Model T log-cutter. This was our low-speed test track.

Best of all, the exit ramp curled down off Interstate I-95 not a hundred yards from the shop. Five miles north at Foxboro the highway was closed off. From there all the way to Boston all four lanes had been paved but not scheduled to open for another year. A closed course for land-speed record attempts, if ever there was one, courtesy of the Commonwealth of Massachusetts. This was our high-speed test track.

Like I said, we were sitting there in the crisp November night admiring our shiny cars, drinking coffee the consistency of road tar and comparing the driving ability of Mike Hawthorn and Jean Behra, about which none of us knew anything at all except for the lies Bernard Cahier fed us in the obscure pages of *Road & Track*. The inevitable argument was just dwindling away when the faraway, loon-like wail of tortured tires pierced even the rusted tin walls of the Ripley shed. Somebody was haulin' ass down the exit ramp in full-flail, locked into a high-speed, four-wheel drift. It had to be Mark Silvers.

As knowledgeable spectators at our home track, we could tell right away that he wasn't going to make it. No way. Sure enough, we all trooped outside in a flurry of spilled coffee and three-legged chairs just in time to see a pair of headlights bobble into the air as he lost it and bounced over the curb on the outside of the ramp. When he pancaked into 29, both lights shattered with a hearty whomph. But it was easy to follow his progress. The trail of spark from the dragging bumper went...yep, knew it all along...right into the Great Attleboro Swamp. The steam cloud when the overheated radiator hit the icy water was a hell of an effect, really.

It took Clarence a couple of weeks to get Mark's Corvette dried out, but except that the black carpets were always greenish after that and the waffle-pattern door panels were a bit warped, it came out pretty good, considering. The first thing we did was take it up on the Interstate to "blow the carbon out."

I don't know where he ever thought it had a chance to get loaded up, but Mark could be persuasive when he wanted. Off we went into the teeth of a December snow storm, raging up the unused Interstate.

At eighty, black smoke started coming out the duals. At ninety, we had sparks; at a hundred, great burning chunks of carbon swirling fifty feet behind us. Up around a hundred and twenty, the ignition started breaking up so badly it wouldn't go any faster, even though Mark had both feet on the pedal and was beating on the steering wheel with his fists.

We went all the way into Brookline that way. He only spun twice in the snow, I will say that for him, and both times he managed a neat carom shot off a snowbank to get us straightened out. How was he to know there was a parked car under all that piled-up powder? This time it took Clarence closer to a month to paste all the pieces back together.

Silvers and Moore lived in a tiny saltbox house in the middle of a big alfalfa field. Besides them, there were two girlfriends, four guitars, a flute, the world's loudest continuously playing hi-fi, three scruffy siamese cats and enough fake Ye Olde Colonial furniture to start a Provincetown tourist shop...which is what Mark's mother had done with the rest of it.

Mark was a good six foot two, two hundred pounds, with a head of disreputable black hair that occassionally was featured in the local Op-Ed pages along with other affronts to public decency. His girlfriend Susan was thin, but even taller than he was, with shiny dark hair down to her waist and prep school manners calculated to let you know she had more money than God. Her father owned TWA or something. Susan hated me on sight.

She hated Moore, too. Moore was a scrawny little folksinger, five foot six, maybe, a hundred and twenty pounds, with a wispy little beard. He lived on an exorbitant allowance from his Great Aunt Grace in Shaker Heights. Moore's girlfriend Ricki was an art major at Wheaton, where they kept that mock Gothic gate. She had the most gorgeous straight blonde hair and eyes that were so dark it was like looking into a reflecting pool. She made my tongue feel all swollen whenever I had to talk to her and more than once I had to leave the room to keep from pouncing on her right in front of everybody. She knew it, of course, and teased me unmercifully.

Ricki also had a vocabulary that would make a sailor blush and from Moore's off-hand observations and perpetually hang-dog expression, I got the impression she was damn near insatiable. I was so consumed with passion and jealousy I turned green and purple just at the thought of her.

Ricki drank a quart of rum a day straight from the bottle with no noticeable effect, skied, sailed, shot skeet and pinball like a champ and drove a right-hand drive Elva, the first Elva Courier in the country. Her father had bought it in England from Frank Nichols himself, and even with a little MGA engine she could consistently blow the doors off Moore's big Healey on any road he cared to name. It drove him crazy.

By April, Mark's Vette was on its last legs. Which was actually pretty good for him. His previous MGA had lasted exactly two and a half weeks before it simply refused to start. Nothing Clarence could do would convince that car that life with Mark could be better than death and dismemberment at the scrapper's. Finally, Silvers sold it for seventy-five dollars to some kid who dropped a Chrysler Hemi and 2-speed PowerFlite into it. Flat ruined the car.

Anyway, after a winter of sitting outside without a top, with both front fenders splintered and the windshield cracked, his poor Corvette was looking a little the worse for wear. Definitely not up to our group's high standards by any means. After a few pointed remarks, Mark stopped coming by Clarence's except when he had to.

That Vette already had sixty thousand miles on it, though, which was pretty impressive considering it'd spent at least a third of its young life sitting at Clarence's with the hood open. Mark and I thought nothing of driving from Providence to Ogunquit for an afternoon of early season surfing, for example. And Ogunquit is in Maine.

The car kept looking worse and worse until Moore and Ricki got drunk one night on Tequila, bought about two dozen spray cans at Montgomery-Ward's and painted the poor thing a particularly virulent shade of chartreuse metalflake...chrome, seats, windshield and all.

Mark just wrapped a rag around his fist, busted out the windshield so he could see and continued driving it. In his own peculiar way, he really loved that car. But if it couldn't be perfect, he was determined to flog the hell out of it. There was a lot of symbolic masochism mixed in there that we didn't get to until next semester in Psych 403. I was trying to graduate this semester and I didn't want to even think about it.

Susan was beside herself, of course. *Apoplectic.* She had some idea in the back her mind about presenting Mark to Daddums or something, and she was desperately trying to clean up his act. Mark knew what she was up to, and he made a point of keeping well out of her way.

We had some magic weekends that spring, anyway. A crew-cut friend of mine named Hal Brandt was racing a weird C-modified he'd built in his suburban backyard. It had started life as a doughty Chevrolet station wagon, but Brandt put a home-made fiberglass body on it that looked...well, ugly doesn't really begin to say it, really. Like a giant gray lump of Play-Dough some Brobdignagian toddler had thrown down and stepped on in disgust.

I remember it had a grille made out of rusty expanded metal with hexagonal holes in it. And that was the pretty part. Running in C-modified, Brandt had trouble getting under the H-production record at Lime Rock. God that car was slow. Maybe it was because Mark and I were all the pit crew he could wrangle. And he had to promise us free beer.

Mark's Corvette got sicker and sicker. We took to using my shiny little red TD for surfing trips to Newport, with Susan crammed into that little shelf behind the seats, sandals hanging out one side, long hair out the other, with our boards sticking straight up in the air and channelling a sixty-mile-an-hour gale down on top of her. How she hated me and my shiny little red car! Somehow, in her mind I was at the root of all Mark's rotten ways, though Lord knows I was just an innocent bystander.

The weekend before graduation, he and I motored out Route 44 to Thompson Raceway to watch Brandt win his class, for once. Carl Fisher, Peter Goddard, Dwayne Moore and a bunch of us were there, raising hell until well after midnight in a German beer hall out on Route 6 called *Das Brauhaus*. The party broke up when Mark hammered Brandt's silver trophy bowl down over some girl's head and her boyfriend hit Moore a mean chop with a half-empty bottle of Lowenbrau.

On the way back, we folded the TD's windshield down, took off our blood and beer-soaked shirts and let the wind whip us dry as we flew through the dark and silent picture postcard villages trying vainly to catch Moore's Healey. We finally passed him when he got lost going through Providence, and so we were leading when we hit South Attleboro about three in the morning.

You'd know the sound anywhere. I dutifully stopped at the intersection next to Clarence's. Mark and Moore lived off the swamp, and over the sound of my puny stock exhaust we could hear the wail of an engine. A V-8 engine. A Corvette V-8 engine somewhere the wrong side of the redline. It was spilling its guts out in an alfalfa field next to the swamp. When we got there, Susan and Ricki were sitting on the porch sharing a quart of Bacardi and waiting for Mark's car to die.

They'd filled the tank, put a huge rock on the gas pedal, tied the steering wheel to full left lock and popped it into First. The Vette had been grinding a skidpad circle in the field for hours, and they couldn't believe anything would run that long with the valves hitting the piston tops.

Mark never said a word, just hopped in Moore's Healey. They cut a ragged one-eighty across the lawn as Moore headed out to the highway. We could hear them as they went overhead on the Interstate, Dwayne winding it out in top and then holding it open until we couldn't hear them any more over the racket from Mark's circling car.

The next morning, I got there about noon, my head throbbing in the sun. The sorry wreck of Mark's dead Vette was sitting in a foot-deep circular trench in the middle of the field. Ricki's dirty Elva was nuzzled up to the porch and Moore's road-weary Healey was lounging in the driveway. Dwayne and the girls were sitting on the porch, sipping herbal tea. He'd dropped Mark off in Harvard Square about five in the morning, said Moore, and Silvers had told him to get lost.

We were all laying on a blanket behind the house drinking rum and coke when we heard the tires squeal down the ramp. Not loudly, mind you, not violently, but quickly. The hair behind my ear felt all prickly, for some reason, and it wasn't because Ricki had me rubbing suntan oil into her back. Nobody thought much about it until the car pulled off 29, across the swamp road and into the driveway.

It was Mark, of course. And he had another Corvette, obviously brand-new, gleaming black with silver stripes on the sides, even skinny whitewall tires and those funny knock-off wheelcovers Corvettes came with then. It was gorgeous and it couldn't have had fifty miles on it. The dealer's price sticker was still pasted to the window. Next to Ricki, I've never coveted anything so much in my life before or since.

I stopped rubbing Ricki's back to watch as Mark opened the passenger door. He took out a big cardboard box, turned to us and made a small, elegant bow to Susan. She was sitting there with her mouth open. Then he laughed, a manic, wild, scary laugh. He reached into the box and produced a spray can. "No...Mark...No!" But he was already painting the windshield. Chartreuse metalflake.

Muscle Car Outrage

The first time one of us got nailed right there on Interstate 95 was a shock. A shock? It was an *outrage*. Tony was just tootling home from work in his GT-350 Shelby with the fat tires and the blue-tinted windows, minding his business as always, when suddenly out of nowhere the gumball machine appeared and he got an $80 ticket. Then Steve got nailed in his 426 Hemi Satellite GTX and it was even box stock—almost invisible—on the outside. His ticket was 94 mph and $90. Incredible. This had never happened to us before. I mean. we were *immune*.

Total panic. From all reports, you'd be driving along and before you even had a chance to spot them pacing you, the lights were flashing and the sirens blaring. I drove our favorite 10-mile stretch of Interstate from Providence to Warwick twice every night to work and I started slowing down to 80 or so and looking carefully for some sort of new cop hiding places. Never saw anything and then, *zap*, just like the others, they had my '66 GTO convertible over in the gravel writing out a pink slip. Drove me wild.

Steve and I talked to a couple of the guys we knew on the force, off-duty of course. Bought them beers and spaghetti down at Smith's on Atwells Avenue, even. But every time we edged the conversation towards the mysterious tickets we'd been getting, these two birds would just smile secret smiles to each other and start talking about how it looked like the Red Sox were going to be hopeless again this summer. We took to driving down I-95 in two cars a half-mile apart to see what we could see. Nothing.

And then Bobby made the papers. Bobby had this bent 427 Corvette he'd bought from a kid up at Brown, some senator's brat who'd wrecked the thing the week after he got it. Bobby spent three months working every night after his shop closed to get a new body onto it. And what the hell. Guy spends all that time and money working on his car, he wants to see what it'll do. Right? According to the cops, what Bobby's Corvette would do was 136 mph, a $200 fine, a disorderly conduct charge and a six-month suspended sentence.

We still wouldn't have known what was going on except Bobby got so mad when they pulled him over without warning that he took a swing at the cop, and the cop slugged him and brought him down to night court in handcuffs. *Handcuffs*, for Chrissake. And of course, that made the *Providence Journal* on page three, along with this story about the newfangled radar unit the police had bought. It was the first in New England, they said.

R a d a r. In 1967, radar was something they

used in Viet Nam to land fighter planes on aircraft carriers. All we knew about radar was that it was definitely dangerous to your health to be anywhere near where they needed radar to do anything. But we also knew that radar was for using against enemies of the free world, not against kids in Providence. That was like ordering B-52s to bomb wattle and daub villages...sheer overkill.

But worse, it was an insult to our sporting instincts. The rules of the game had been changed in mid-stream, without even warning the players. That's what got to us most. It was so *sneaky*.

We still weren't sure what we were looking for, but we piled in my GTO—Cragar mags, redline Tiger Paws, white over white with red bucket seats, engine by Milt Schornack at Royal Pontiac—put the top down so we could see better and cruised very slowly along the Interstate. It took us three passes before we noticed the plain Ford Galaxie wagon parked on the Airport Road overpass. There were two Providence cops sitting up there fiddling with a big box in the back. And right on the other side, they had a Dodge chase car hidden behind a newly-planted row of hemlocks, with a gravel drive that connected to the on-ramp. Very clever.

We went down and turned around and checked out the other side. And Steve, who went to art school, started making a map of the whole area...the highway, the overpass, the on-ramps, the "for official use only" turn-around across the median. He even made me drive up and stop next to the plainclothes wagon so he could eye-ball the setup. And then of course, the cops wanted to know what we were doing.

Wouldn't you know, it was Flanagan and Bracco,

the same two we'd bought lunch.

"What you boys doing," said Flanagan, "admiring our new toy?" And then he laughed.

"Kinda takes the sport out, don't it?" said Bracco.

And then, because they were trying to be our friends and save us from a life of crime and all, the two of them loosened up and showed us how their radar worked. We were very polite and looked everything over, nodding at all the right places in Flanagan's memorized talk.

"Just about every big-wig in the State Senate has been down to see how this baby works," he said proudly. "They're thinking about getting a whole bunch more. Maybe that'll slow you guys down." And he laughed again.

"Very nice," said Steve. "But you know what they say about radar. It makes you sterile." Bracco already had four kids with the fifth on the way.

"Then again," said Steve perfectly straight-faced, "are you sure your wife didn't ask Commissioner Kelly to assign you to this thing? I saw her and Mrs. Kelly talking together in DiLorenzo's Market a couple weeks ago." And with that, I laid a patch about 20 feet long by way of saying good-bye.

"Hey...get back here, you bastards." cried Bracco. Flanagan just laughed.

Steve didn't say anything more until we were safely ensconsed in the back booth at Smith's, a round of 'Gansetts making beery circles on the polished black marble table top.

"Very clever," said Steve. "But not clever enough."

Everybody looked confused, except for Bobby who was still nursing his sore jaw with the back of his hand and eyeing Ellen, the only decent looking waitress in Smith's.

"Look," said Steve. "We don't have to race on I-95. Right? We don't even have to drive on I-95. We can go around them. But don't you understand? That's what they want us to do. Pretty soon, they're gonna have those radar units all over town and we're not gonna be able to back out of the driveway. Right?"

He took another slug of halfwarm beer.

"If we let them get away with this, pretty soon every decent dragging road we've got will be too hot to race on and then where will we be?"

The table pondered this question in morose silence, not even perking up when I waved for a cold round of 'Gansetts.

"But you, of course, have a plan," I said as sarcastically as I could.

"Damn right. If we can make that radar trap look like a joke, if we can get the politicians convinced that it's not worth the trouble, or even better, that their precious radar trap is *encouraging* people to speed, then maybe they'll leave us alone."

Bobby reluctantly turned around from watching Ellen bend over in her mini-skirt to set down a platter of pizza across the room.

"How you gonna do that, smartass?" And he let out a small garlic flavored burp to emphasize his point.

"What we're gonna do is run a few drag races on I-95. And the guy with the fastest car wins the pot. Here's my 50." And he laid a $50 bill on the spilled beer.

"Get your money up. Tony's the treasurer."

"This guy is nuts," Bobby announced, standing up in the booth so the restaurant patrons could hear him better. "He's crazy."

"Crazy like a fox," I said, peeling off tens. "There's $50 that says 400 cubic inches from Royal Pontiac eats Ramcharger Hemi Plymouths for breakfast."

Obviously, Steve had figured out a way to get through the speed trap without getting caught. If he'd lead, I'd follow. Figuratively, that is. I knew my GTO could beat his skinny ass anytime, anywhere.

"We better have a time limit," I said as Ellen came over with our tray of beers. Tony had his hand on Bobby's shoulder to hold him down if he tried to jump Ellen, but Bobby was too busy trying to follow Steve's idea. Ellen looked hurt and stomped away with the empties. Steve licked his lips as he watched her go.

"I say the fastest run by the end of the month wins the pot," said Steve. "That'll give us three weeks."

"I humbly suggest since nobody asked me," I said, "that we open this competition to all comers. Anybody who's got $50 bucks and a fast car can run. I also suggest we appoint my buddy George Park, who just happens to be the most listened-to disc jockey on WPLJ six-fifty on your dial, to be our chairman of publicity."

"Motion carried. Bobby buys the next round."

The next Wednesday night, we met at Bobby's body shop, down in the Italian ghetto right off Route 6. He was busy priming the nose of a low-mileage Eldorado that had been stolen and pushed into a culvert. His brother the insurance adjuster had sold the "totalled" Eldo to Bobby for peanuts. All it needed was a paint job.

We waited patiently around until the primer was on, eating black cherry-filleds from the Dunkin' Donuts next door and pointing out invisible dust marks to the short tempered painter. When Steve got there, we went out in the dark, and smoked cigarettes, and stood with our hands in our pockets, talked in low voices and scraped our pointy toe boots around in the gravel. Mostly we stared silently at the car.

Steve's Hemi GTX was dark red with a black interior...the base stripper model. But the rear end was jacked up, the chassis was painted white and so were the wide steel wheels he'd had built by a guy who did wheels for oval track racers. He had Mickey Thompson tires on it, and a Hurst shifter. That was all you could see from outside.

Under the hood was a full-house NASCAR 426 Hemi that was maybe the strongest motor between Boston and New York. But I knew he was running 4.88 gears in it and unless he'd changed them there was no way he'd go faster than maybe 120, tops. I also noticed his "Discover Rhode Island" license plates had been swapped for some New York plates I'd never seen before.

When Bobby was finally done, about midnight, we convoyed down to I-95. I drove down the course first, to make sure there were no drunks or idiots in the way. And of course, since this was to be a timed run, to make sure our unsuspecting timers were set up tonight. I also wanted to make sure George the DJ was up there interviewing Flanagan for WPLJ so we'd be sure to get the timing slip from the tower.

George's clapped-out Falcon was sitting at the end of the overpass with the dome light on. That could mean only one thing. Race Time.

Just like we used to do in the pre-radar days, Steve and I did a rolling start a mile up the road from the overpass. At about 30, Tony waved his handkerchief out my passenger window and Steve was gone in a squeal of tires and a cloud of white smoke. That Hemi sounded fine, I must admit. I rolled along at 60, not wanting to upset the radar beam. We really wanted Flanagan to lock in on Steve...which was a pretty funny feeling.

But it wasn't half as funny as Bracco's chase car stuck through a hemlock hedge. By the time we rolled innocently beneath the overpass, Steve was nowhere to be seen. But DJ George was interviewing Flanagan about what had happened, live on the radio. Bracco stomped around kicking gravel in the air.

The gist of the interview was that some dope-crazed hippie in a racing car had come through the radar trap at 124 mph and Officer Bracco who was driving the chase car at the time had become so excited he'd gotten his 426 Hemi Dodge police cruiser completely crossed up in the loose gravel and fish-tailed through the hemlock hedge backwards. Then he'd got it stuck in the fresh sod trying to accelerate out again. That's when George burst out laughing right on the radio and somebody back in the studio had enough sense to hit the button to start the Beatles' *Fool on the Hill.*

The next morning, the *Providence Journal* ran a full column about the "criminal drivers" that had offered a $1000 prize for the fastest car clocked through the I-95 police radar.

"It's the thrill of beating that radar trap that makes it worthwhile," the *Journal* quoted an anonymous street racer. "Without that radar unit, who'd want to race?" The story was signed by the Providence AP stringer, one George H. Park.

I had volunteered to be second through the traps, knowing it was going to be interesting, to say the least. But I figured I not only had the fastest car, but the lowest number of points on my license. And if it came to that, I also had the father with the most bail money. Having been there the night before and gotten an exclusive eye-witness scoop, it was only natural for George to stop by to check out the action. And then of course, he stopped by to tell us.

"Ah yes," said DJ George (he had a W.C. Fields fixation). "You're not going to believe this, my little Chickadees, but there must be twenty serious street racers sitting on Washington Street waiting for good Officer Flanagan to assemble his mysterious machinery. And our poor friends Bracco and Flanagan have two city councilmen, Lieutenant Coffee and three state senators up there to observe the efficacy of their police performance. Bracco is so nervous he can't even talk."

"What about media? " asked Steve.

"Ah yes, the fourth estate. Me, the UPI guy and two local TV stations."

"I love it. We better get down to Washington Street and get this organized before those guys get themselves a bunch of tickets. Bracco may be dumb, but he can drive pretty good."

On the way through the dark side streets, I took the opportunity to wing it, just once. Tony and

I had spent the afternoon swapping my usual 4.11 gears for a set of 3.07s. The old low-speed punch was gone, of course, but I figured this was a top speed run. With a little luck, I could probably outrun Bracco's Hemi police cruiser if I had to. I tugged at my seatbelt, checked my instruments, rapped it one last time to make sure the plugs were clean, squirmed down in the seat and figured I was as ready as I'd ever be.

Tony rode with Bobby in the Corvette, running quietly along at 40. We came down off the Washington Street ramp with the Corvette and me side-by-side, all alone on the Interstate. Tony leaned out the passenger window, checked fore and aft and waved his handkerchief.

Waaugh. WAAUGH. W A A U G H. I had Second until 80, Third over 100, then foot to the floor in Fourth. For a tall rear end, she was doing fine. I flashed under the bridge at 5500 rpm, somewhere around 130. As I went by, I checked the hemlock hedge. Nobody.

And then I checked my mirrors for the first time. Bracco's Dodge cruiser was only a couple hundred yards behind me, lights flashing angrily. The siren was probably wailing, but I couldn't hear it over my own engine. He must have started when he first saw me coming, because not even Steve's Hemi was that quick off the line. Oh *shit.*

Bracco was sticking with me, or maybe even gaining a little. There was nothing else to do but keep my foot on the floor and head for the Warwick city line, 10 miles down the road. There was no traffic around at all, except for a group of cars in the right hand lane that I seemed to be catching a lot more slowly than I should. The tach needle was still against the peg and Bracco was now maybe an eighth-mile behind me. Finally, I edged by the fast-running cars in the slow lane. They must have been doing 110, easy.

As I went by, one set of lights pulled into the center lane, another into the fast lane. There were now cars occupying all three lanes, and a fourth running along the break-down lane. And Bracco was somewhere behind them, fishtailing to beat hell as he tried to get a full-size Dodge police car—which didn't have very good brakes—slowed down from 130 without running into the solid, perfectly legal, 70 mph barrier in front of him. I tried to see what was going on, but all I could make out was a rapidly diminishing pack of lights in my mirrors.

Headlights out, I motored along back streets to Bobby's shop to wait for the rest of the guys. Bobby and Tony showed up first, laughing to beat hell. Then Steve pulled softly into the lot and smiled. Behind him came a regular procession of Hemi Dodges and Plymouths, 442s and 396 Chevelles, a bunch of Camaros and Mustangs, a couple Corvettes and even some guy in a Cobra roadster. At the very back was DJ George, waving his reporter's notebook.

"Red hot race results straight from the timing tower," he said.

"How'd I do?" I asked.

"Second out of twenty-three. The guy in the Cobra blew your doors off." I guess I must have looked confused.

"While dear Bracco was off chasing you," he said, "Tony ran everybody else through Flanagan's radar trap. Ah yes. Officer Flanagan look it very badly, I'm afraid. The poor man locked himself in Councilman Agostino's Cadillac and refused all our entreaties to come out. So Lieutenant Coffee and I ran the radar."

"What happened to Bracco?"

"Ah yes, Officer Bracco. Bracco was last seen cruising the empty freeway by himself, having been left there by four young hooligans in high-powered cars who accelerated rapidly off an exit ramp near Warwick and eluded all attempts at pursuit. Such is life for the hardworking Guardian of the Law. And now, if you'll excuse me, I must away to my copy desk to make you all famous. No names, of course."

"I figure this'll keep things lively for a couple weeks," announced Steve loudly enough for everyone to hear.

"Meet me back here, two weeks from tonight. And bring anybody you can find who's got a fast car. The more the merrier." And with that, he drove off into the night.

"No doubt working on some fiendish scheme to get us all five-to-ten with no probation," said Tony.

"Something like that," I said, still smarting over being whipped by a college kid in a Cobra.

"I wouldn't drive your car much for a while if I were you."

"Likewise, I'm sure," said Tony, bowing as well as he could from the driver's seat of his Shelby Mustang.

"See you at Smith's." And then he dropped the clutch and got rubber all the way down the block.

The storm that broke the next day was even bigger than before, of course. We made all the local papers and radio news shows. Both TV stations showed high-speed headlights zooming past the camera and Officer Flanagan pouting before Councilman Agostino read a statement off the teleprompter about the silliness of using a radar trap as a deterrent to speeding and the stupidity of wasting taxpayer's good money on such a blue-sky scheme when school lunch programs were underfinanced. Agostino owned the biggest dairy in Rhode Island.

By the next night, the overpass on I-95 looked like an armed camp. Lieutenant Coffee now had four pursuit cars stationed there and two more assigned as a road block a few miles further down the road. He probably would have had the National Guard, too, but they were busy waiting for a race riot to start downtown.

But except for a stray drunk or two and an occasional high school kid, they didn't catch anybody for almost a week. And then, just about the time they'd relaxed, a black Corvette, or at least that's what they thought it might have been, ripped off a 142 mph run, dived down the exit ramp and was gone before the chase cars could get mobilized.

"God, I hate them little Cobras," said Bobby into the eternal darkness of Smith's back room, his eyes permanently attached to Ellen's tightly packaged form.

"Your turn to buy."

The next night, according to the newspapers, some guy on an antique Vincent Black Shadow was clocked at 133, which was pretty good for an old motorcycle. He escaped by diving through a hole in the median divider, going half-a-mile down the wrong side of the freeway and up an on-ramp.

Councilman Agostino called for Police Commissioner Kelly's resignation, a law banning radar in the state and a free milk program in the schools. The Letters to the Editor column was solidly anti-radar too, written by concerned citizens who were afraid of getting run over by drag racers who had been tempted to race by the city's radar unit. This was better than Steve had hoped.

We assembled at Bobby's around 10 pm. It was going to be the biggest party anybody had been to all summer, and nobody wanted to miss it. We counted 128 cars, and a few more trickled in later on. Every hot car in Providence was there, all the way from high-schoolers in Daddy's 440 Chrysler Wedge to some guy in a converted Comet Funny Car. Steve assigned guards to close off the street for two blocks in either direction, and lectured the crowd from the back of Bobby's El Camino parts hauler.

With much laughing and joking and revving of engines, the largest ever meeting of Providence musclecars split up and drove at one-minute intervals down three different routes. It was like playing Green Berets in guerrilla warfare.

"No use attracting attention until you want it," said Steve.

We quietly assembled—as quietly as 130 street racers can assemble—in a high school parking lot just two blocks from our favorite Washington Street on-ramp. Occasionally, you could hear traffic going by on the elevated Interstate, and the whole area of town had a yellowish tinge from the arc lights. But there didn't seem to be anybody around to bother us.

"Whaddaya got in the box?" asked Bobby.

"I'd like you to meet our secret weapon," said

Steve, pointing to an enclosed trailer parked in the high school shadows.

"This is my friend Duncan." Steve opened the trailer door with a flourish.

"And this is the fastest Group 7 Can-Am car in the Northeast. It's called a Lola, and anyone who even breathes on it gets his arm ripped off at the socket."

Well. We all stood around and watched as Steve and this Duncan character rolled this far-out, bright blue and yellow racing car off the trailer. About the only part I could recognize was its 427 Chevy motor. The steering wheel was even on the right. Duncan wedged himself into this projectile, and Steve pushed it single-handedly to the head of the line, through a double row of openmounted wonder. When Duncan reached down and found his metallic blue helmet to put on, I thought I'd faint. These guys were *serious*.

They fired that thing up, and you could see lights flick on all over the neighborhood. I thought I had a hot car. *Hah*. This Lola made my GTO sound like a milk truck. Duncan spurted ahead in that spastic way that funny cars and dragsters have, but with a lot more control, it seemed like. What I wouldn't give to be driving that, which is what every one of the guys was thinking, I could tell.

Duncan went as slowly as he could up the on-ramp, while the rest of us formed dozens of three-by-three rows. Steve's Hemi was in the front row with Bobby's Corvette and some guy's 442 Olds. Tony's Shelby, the Cobra roadster and my GTO were the rear guard. In between, there were more street racers than anybody could believe. It looked like the pits at Raceway Park before the Summernationals.

The guys were all smiling at each other and looking around, like kids on Christmas morning. All up and down the lines, you could see these heads bobbing up and down, excited and scared.

DJ George was up on the overpass with Lieutenant Coffee, and he said the noise was unbelievable. Like a squadron of B-24s taking off. And then out of the pack, the dark blue Lola came roaring with breathtaking speed. The radar went off the dial at 150, and the Lola was still accelerating when the radar simply gave a sigh and stopped recording, a small whisper of gray smoke going up from the back of it.

The four chase cars were all over each other trying to get down their ramp to go after Duncan, and they got into a minor multi-car fender-bender before they got straightened out. By the time Coffee could radio his road block, the Lola was already past it. And when the poor lieutenant turned around again, the front row of the world's largest drag race was just passing 100 mph and the overpass at the same time. Coffee sat there with his head in his hands while DJ George broadcast live and tried to take pictures at the same time.

We rolled past the hemlock hedge that still bore the effects of Bracco's maneuver. We rolled past the road block crew, who wisely figured discretion was the better part of valor. Setting up a two-car road block to stop a hundred cars going 120 mph isn't something they teach you at the police academy.

About a half-mile later, the four battered chase cars looked up from their hopeless pursuit of Duncan's Lola only to see a highway full of headlights in their mirrors. Hundreds of fast-moving headlights, covering the whole width of Interstate 95, were rapidly gaining on them. The cops did the only thing they could. They got on those Hemi Dodges for all they were worth and started leading our high-speed parade.

Steve chased them all the way to the Warwick town line before he led us off the exit ramp by the shopping center, around the cloverleaf and back north again. As we went along, cars kept peeling off from the rear, until only the front row was left to go back under the radar overpass, three fast moving street racers occupying the whole road at 120 mph. And then they zapped off, too, first to get Duncan's Lola stuffed back in its trailer and towed to Bobby's shop, then to meet the rest of us at Smith's for the grand prize award ceremony.

Duncan got the $1000 pot by unanimous decision, and then made a hundred friends for life by turning $500 back to buy beer for the assembled multitude. Poor Ellen gave up on trying to keep track of anything. She came over and quietly sat with Bobby for the rest of the night, her arm in his, while we ran a bucket brigade to pass beer mugs to the tap and back to the tables. Smith's well-stocked cellar held out until 4 am. Everyone agreed that it was the best party Smith's had ever seen.

When DJ George came in with the first proofs of tomorrow's *Journal*, it was like getting the early reviews of your new Broadway show, sitting in Vince Sardi's. George got a standing ovation, particularly when he announced that he'd called the Governor and gotten him out of bed, told him what happened and got a taped interview which he'd quoted in the paper. And then he read it out loud to us.

"Governor Chapin told this reporter in an exclusive interview, 'After our terrible experience with this speed-tempting police radar, I can't imagine it will ever be used anywhere, in any state, ever again.'"

Never again. Ah yes.

Shit Happens

I always check the odometer on the grid. Twenty laps of Lime Rock is 30.6 miles, and I want to know when the race is almost over. We don't have a pitboard, and the starter never bothers give us a white flag for "one more lap to go." The grid steward holds up a finger meaning "one minute" and hops over the barrier. Up on the tower, the starter raises his green flag. I stick it into gear, bring the revs up to 4000 rpm on the tach, and dump the clutch as the flag falls.

As usual, I've qualified poorly, and my big V-8 is quicker than the cars around me. I dart right, go down the inside along the grass, and pick up four places before I'm out of second gear. I catch third just before the hairpin, and squeeze inside an old red Corvette trying to cut across my bow. I go wide in front of him, then cut back to the second apex and chop him off. He taps me up the ass as we go into the esses, just to let me know he's pissed.

Fender to fender, nose to tail, we wobble and

slide on cold Blue Streaks through the esses and onto the short chute. I pick off an XKE going into the uphill, hold him off down the back straight, and almost pile into the traffic jam in front of me as some asshole in a Daimler roadster jams on his brakes going down the hill under the bridge. I manage to get straightened out onto the front straight, and already, the pack is stringing out.

Five or six cars ahead, I can see Timmy and Matt, side by side into the hairpin. Timmy tries to outbrake him on the inside, and instead goes straight on into the grass in a cloud of tire smoke and dust. As I power by, the chrome yellow Sting Ray is gracefully spinning around for the third time, but on a trajectory that will take it past the end of the bank, past the flag station with its anxiously waving yellow flag, and onto the grass. No big deal. All he has to do is keep the clutch in, keep the engine running and catch it as it comes around. But by then I'll be long gone.

Timmy owns a speed shop on Long Island. He's got this mechanic named Roger, who's a wacky eccentric—talking like Donald Duck to preferred customers is the most *normal* of his behavior patterns—but who is the best Corvette mechanic on the East Coast. He used to run a NASCAR team down south, and the first thing he did when he moved North was build Timmy's '65 Coupe into a car that was so good they won the Northeast Championship in a walk-away.

It doesn't hurt that Timmy has been around Lime Rock, Thompson, Watkins Glen and Bridgehampton literally thousands of times in the ten years since he started racing, that he's absolutely fearless, and that he has incredible car control. He doesn't have a clue as to why he goes so fast, and he doesn't know anything at all about cars. He's just a *natural*.

Matt is some sort of rich middle-age industrialist...he's always just flying back from Germany or Hong Kong or South America, but he never wants to talk about just what it is that he does. According to Roger, when Matt started racing he was hopeless. Then about three years ago, he suddenly figured it all out, and now he's almost as fast as Timmy.

He's got an identical Sting Ray, except that Tim's is always filthy and banged up, with numbers made from silver tape and patches sprayed with dull gray primer. It's a classic case of the shoemaker's children...the last car to get prepped is the shop owner's, and there's never time for niceties like fresh paint. Matt's coupe is always immaculate, and he's the only one of us with permanently-painted numbers...dark blue to contrast with his white car.

As the race settles down, the white blur of his tail is just far enough in front of me that I can see it turning into the hairpin as I'm halfway down the main straight. Timmy is nowhere in sight behind me, but I know he's driving like hell to catch up, because he's no longer in the grass by the hairpin and there's dirt and gravel spread around at every apex. You know when Timmy's really flying, because he's got two wheels off on every corner and the track is littered with debris.

Roger claims my Daytona Blue '64/'67 Sting Ray coupe is the best car he's ever built...even slicker than Timmy's. He calls it a Four-Seven, because I rammed somebody in a Jaguar in practice at Bridgehampton in July, and the only fenders we could get quickly were a pair of '67s the local body-shop had ordered for some girl who'd sideswiped a telephone pole with her brand-new roadster. We pop-rivetted the '67 fenders onto my '64, threw some bondo over the rivets and some spray paint over the bondo, and that's the way I'm still driving it.

Tim's shop sponsors all three cars...in the sense that Matt and I pay for all our own damage, but Roger maintains the cars for free. Timmy drives the car the way Roger sets it up. Matt knows enough to be always changing shock absorbers or fiddling with spring spacers or wanting different tires. He drives Roger crazy, and half the time, they switch back to what they started with before the race itself.

This is only my second year racing, so I depend on Roger to tell me what to do. I'm not as consistent as Timmy and Matt—and I still have trouble getting up for qualifying—but on my occassional good days I can run with either of them. The highpoint of my season so far was qualifying on the outside pole, with Matt next to me and Timmy right behind. They drove away from me as soon as the flag dropped, but for one brief shining moment, there, I thought Camelot was in Connecticut.

Still, the situation is like this. There's a ten-race series for the Northeast Championship. I've got a string of seconds and thirds; Matt and Timmy have either won or crashed trying. So starting in April and racing till October, we've come out within a couple of points of each other. Whoever finishes ahead of the other two in today's race will win the Championship, and the $1000 season prize. It doesn't matter if any of us wins the race, just where we finish in relationship to each other.

I can just barely see Timmy in my mirrors as I come down the straight. There are still two cars between us, but he's catching me perhaps a second or two each lap. In front, Matt's white car has mysteriously slowed. He's racing nose-to-tail with a dark blue Cobra, and the traffic that was separating us has passed them. There's nothing between Matt and me except a 427 Cobra and about two seconds of air, and I'm closing that gap.

Another couple of laps, and Timmy and I have sneaked past the Cobra. Matt is right in front of me, while Timmy is on my tail. Going down the straight, I check the odometer...30 miles. This is the last lap! I inch my way up to Matt's bumper, and outbrake him into the hairpin. His brakes have obviously faded, because there's nothing he can do. Timmy passes Matt coming into the esses, which slows him down a bit and gives me a second or two to catch my breath.

All I have to do is hold Timmy off up the hill, into west bend, under the bridge, down the straight...and there's no checkered flag! I must have been so nervous, I checked the odometer *before* the warm-up lap. This isn't fair. I've had all I could do to hold Timmy off for one lap. I can't manage another.

A yellow fender slowly grows in my right side window as we go into the hairpin. We brake side by side, downshift simultaneously, and I chop him off with a brutal swerve towards the apex. I can *feel* the grinding of fiberglass as we slide into the turn, his front fender rubbing my rear wheel. I've got the line, though, and there's not much he can do about it.

Timmy is all over me...he tries to go inside and I cut him off. He tries to go left into the esses, and I cut him off again. Down the short chute he feints left and as I block him, he tries to go right. I'm slightly ahead as we brake into the uphill righthander, and as I cut across to the apex Timmy rams me. *Hard*, smack in the passenger door.

I'm spinning, a tight clockwise spiral that sends me toward the guardrail. I look over as I come around again, and there's Timmy's yellow car, not ten yards away, backed into the rail. Even with earplugs and open exhausts, I can hear the fiberglass shatter as I hit the fence. Matt's white coupe is just coming into view around the corner, and he dives to the right side of the track to get as far away from the accident as possible.

My car bounces off the rail and back onto the track, as I jam the lever into first and pop the clutch. My foot is still hard on the throttle, and the rear wheels break loose completely. I rocket across the course in front of Matt, spin 180 degrees in the grass on the other side, and start back onto the asphalt. He obviously has no idea where my car is headed, and neither do I.

Matt tries to avoid me, but the right side of his car slices the nose clean off my Corvette. I can see the headlights and grille go spiralling over the top of his hood. Then he's past. The impact has stopped me dead in the center of the track, engine still running, car in gear, my feet on the clutch and the brakes. I'm getting a bit dazed, at this point. Now, first I'll put my foot on the gas, then I'll let out the clutch, and...

Cobra! The dark blue 427 roadster comes up the blind hill to find me sideways across the track.

Oh...*shit*. He smashes point blank into my driver's side door, and crystals of broken glass and fiberglass float around inside my coupe like snow in one of those plastic paperweights with the Santa Claus inside. He careens off into the guardrail, head first.

My engine is *still* running, and my mind is pumped full of adrenalin. If I just can get another quarter-mile, it says, I'll beat Timmy and finish second behind Matt for the championship. I crank it hard right and roar down the back straight, around west bend, under the bridge and down the main straight to take the checkered flag from an obviously confused starter. Roger is standing with his stop-watch dangling at his side, his mouth hanging open. Two of his cars have come around as rolling wrecks, and the third one hasn't shown at all.

I do my cool off lap with the temperature gauge soaring, bits of fiberglass and glass blowing off and around me, unusual smells coming from under the hood. The steering pulls hard to the left. Timmy is sitting on the fender of his wreck as I go by. He points, laughs and raises his hands shoulder-high in the New Yorker's universal sign that means "I'm sorry, but what could I do."

Back in the paddock, the reviews are mixed. Timmy is apologetic, because the whole incident was his fault in the first place. "More work for the body shop," I say. Everybody laughs politely. Even though he won, Matt is furious because his immaculate car has been peeled like a grape all the way down the right side, exposing a dirty array of Corvette guts. "Shit Happens," quacks Roger in his Donald Duck voice, which doesn't make Matt any happier.

Then there's the guy in the Cobra, which is now a couple feet shorter than it used to be. Unlike a Corvette, you don't just bond a new fender onto a one-piece aluminum body. We're talking Big Bucks, here. He files a protest with the stewards, and gets a DSQ put next to my name in the race results, which means I don't place in the championship, after all. He also gets my SCCA license suspended for six months. "Reckless endangerment," or something like that, say the stewards. But they've carefully timed it so my sentence is served before the first race of next season.

Every SCCA competition car has a log book that chronicles its every race. The tech inspector writes in mine, "Severe damage to front, rear, left side, right side. Broken windshield and rear window. The top looks okay." My friend Russ the track photographer comes over with a mangled piece of blue fiberglass, one Sting Ray headlight assembly and a twisted grille.

"Here's a gift from the corner workers," he says, and drops the pile on the ground. "Christ, even your seat got bent. You're lucky you got out of that one alive."

"Well," quacks Roger. "Shit Happens."

One Night at Myrna's

The first time I saw Dave's Chevelle, I threw up. In my helmet. I was minding my business in the parking lot of the A&W drive-in, sipping a root beer float. I was sitting there in the darkness on my Honda 175 Scrambler, after washing the mud off at the car wash out by the Mall. I sucked up a big mouthful of soda just as Dave roared up behind me, screeched on the brakes and blew the horn. I jumped probably a foot in the air, spraying creamy vanilla/ root beer mix all over the top of my bike.

Then I turned around to see who the jerk was, and when I saw my best friend behind the wheel of a shiny new 396 Chevelle SS, something kind of caught in the back of my throat. I started coughing, and I couldn't stop. I could feel it rising up in the back of my mouth, and there was nothing I could do. I had already dropped my big soda container. I grabbed my helmet. I half filled it up.

When I was done, I just sat there for a minute, wiping my mouth on the sleeve of my sweatshirt. I could hear Dave laughing and beating on the door of his car with his hand. I reached up, turned on the ignition and kick-started the Honda into its almost inaudible idle. Then I rolled backwards between the shiny black Chevelle and Donnie Howland's chopped '34 Ford three-window.

"Bobby, you little...you wouldn't." Dave could see it coming. He reached across the seat to wind up the passenger window, and I caught him full in the face with the contents of my helmet, followed by the helmet itself. He pawed at the mess on his face and started screaming.

"Don't hurt the car. Please don't hurt the car."

He threw himself out the driver's door, hoping to catch me as I went behind the Chevelle. Instead, I went forward, up over the sidewalk, through the open glass doors on one side of the A&W counter and out the open doors on the other side. A sloppy berm shot off the trash can by the exit, and I caught third gear onto Main Street.

By the time I heard Dave peel out from the parking lot, I was already riding around the back of Myrna Garrison's house on Seventeenth Street. Every light was on, and there were half-a-dozen cars in front of the yard, including the big Mercedes sedan that Ralph DelGrado's stockbroker father let him take to college, Tony's old GTO Pontiac and the inevitable Volkswagen bus covered with plastic flowers and Make Love Not War stickers.

I could see a bunch of people sitting on the floor of the living room, the whole block was pulsating with Janis Joplin screaming *Ball and Chain* and you could smell the sweet funk of pot smoke from the street. It was a typical Saturday night at Myrna's.

I stood in the garden with the hose, and washed off me and the Honda, simultaneously. When I quietly knocked on the kitchen door, Myrna opened it without a word and handed me a big terrycloth robe. I stripped out of my wet clothes in the dark, went in and got a Coke from the refrigerator and padded upstairs. I found some old jeans and a white Obu dashaiki in her closet, and joined the party.

Myrna and her husband were anthropologists teaching at Indiana University, where I was a graduate student. Nobody had ever actually met Dr. Garrison...he had been "on sabbatical" ever since I'd come there. Most of us thought he was a convenient fiction, useful when Myrna wanted to say no...which wasn't very often.

She was maybe thirty at the most, vivacious if not really pretty, and she had cut a wide swath through the male faculty and graduate students. Her ramshackle old Victorian had been turned into the world's longest continuous house party, a place you could go at any time of day or night and be sure of finding cold beer, African Ground Nut Stew so spicey it made your eyes water, recreational drugs from Tijuana Gold to LSD, what the newspapers called Free Love and a lot of fervid anti-establishment conversation.

The student/faculty strike that had shut down the university for the past month, since the shootings at Kent State, had been planned right in this room. When I sat down on the fringe of the group, three of the most notorious radicals were arguing over the speeches they planned to give at tomorrow's rally in support of a Black Power Store in Bloomington that had been firebombed on Wednesday.

I'd heard it all before, a dozen times. I had just about decided to leave, when Dave flung open the front door. He was dripping wet—he must have washed off with Myrna's garden hose the same way I had—and he was hopping mad. A puddle of water quickly formed on Myrna's white carpet from India, the one with embroidered flowers around the edges.

"I thought I'd find you here."

"Hey Dave, I'm sorry. But you made me mad."

"Yeah, but you didn't have to trash my car."

One of the radical leaders broke off from his argument about student rights.

"If you two Stonies want to fight, do it someplace else, okay?"

There was no love lost between students and locals. We called them Hippie, cause most of them were. They called us Stonie, short for Stonecutter, because the only other industry in Bloomington was cutting limestone from the quarries on the edge of town. Just about every building in the county was built of the same bland, light tan limestone. Even the nicest residential neighborhoods had all the cheerful ambience of a maximum security prison.

I was one of the few people around who sort of bridged the town/gown gap. I was a genuine Stonie, and my grandfather still worked for the Indiana Limestone Company and came home every afternoon covered with a pale dust, like brown sugar. I worked afternoons and weekends as a salesman at Mal Terry's Honda Dealership/Firearms and Sporting Goods Store—the downtown motorhead/huntin'/fishin' center—so I knew just about every male in town...and was related to half of them.

But I was also a graduate student in the English Department at IU. Feeling very self-conscious, I had been out there marching in the streets in most of the anti-war, anti-establishment, anti-ROTC, anti-administration protests. The Hippies thought I was a Redneck, but harmless. The Stonies thought I was a Peacenik, but that I'd come to my senses eventually. Dave thought I owed him something.

"What are you gonna do about my car?"

"What about my helmet? It was brand new."

"Look, I told you two, take this outside."

"Okay. Come 'on, Dave. I'll help you clean up. Besides, I want to see your car."

The Chevelle was really pretty...and thanks to me, it was really a mess. We tried dabbing at it with rags from Myrna's garage, but eventually Dave just turned the garden hose on the black vinyl interior. Then I dried it off while he washed out my helmet. The Chevelle had pleated bucket seats with the automatic shifter in a console, a tachometer and an AM/FM radio. I borrowed some Windex and Lysol spray from Myrna's kitchen cabinets, and got rid of most of the water spots...and most of the smell.

After I got the inside dry, I wiped down the outside of the Chevelle as a peace offering. It had five-spoke chrome wheels, Goodyear Wide Oval tires, "SS" in the grille and crossed flags with a 396 emblem on the fender. The window sticker totalled $4048.25.

"Where'd you ever get four-thousand dollars?"

"I saved everything for the past year, and my father co-siqned the note."

"Can you make the payments?"

"Just about. He put it on his insurance, or I couldn't manage."

A burly figure in shoulder-length hair and a leopard-print dashaiki staggered out on the side porch. It wasn't somebody I recognized as one of Myrna's regulars.

"You damn stonies still here?" His voice had the low-pitched, dreamy whine of the confirmed pothead, his voice burned out from too much dope.

"It's about time for you to leave."

He fumbled with his striped button-fly bellbottoms, then pissed a high amber arc down the hood of the Chevelle.

I could see the red blush start up the back of Dave's neck. He looked at the stranger on the porch pissing on his new car, and then he looked at the garden hose in his hand. I could see him make the connection.

Ferocious swearing indicated that he'd hit his target, dead center. Dave hosed the guy from top to bottom with icy well water, and then as he staggered back through the door, still emptying his bladder in an uncontrolled spray, Dave hosed down the whole living room through the open door. He kept at it until the soaking wet group came pouring out the back door, screaming and shouting, carrying Myrna's collection of Masai ceremonial spears that had been decoratively stacked in one corner of the living room.

Myrna poked her head out the upstairs bedroom window. I could see she was naked. Next to her was the startled face of her graduate teaching assistant, a naive lummox from Terre Haute with a body that women died for and no more sense than a dozen eggs. Dave hit him square in the mouth with a stream of water that left him sputtering and gurgling for air and Myrna helpless with laughter.

"Waddya think, Bobby? About time to find another party?"

I was already in the car. A pair of rare Masai artifacts clattered harmlessly against the trunk as Dave cut a muddy trench across the front lawn, bounced over the curb, chopped off a couple of coeds on bicycles and laid rubber for fifty yards. He touched 80 mph before he had to jam on the brakes for the stoplight at State Road 46.

"My bike's back there."

"So go get it."

"Look. I know you think those Hippies are a bunch of wimps, but some of them are pretty mean. I saw them beat the hell out of a campus cop a couple weeks ago. And that thin one with the beard and the love beads? That's Ralph. I know he carries a .38 Special, because he showed it to me one night."

"What do you wanna do?"

"Drive me around the block on Sixteenth. I can cut through the backyards, and probably push my bike down the street without them hearing me. If you hear me start yelling, you better come blasting down Seventeenth Street like John Wayne in *The Sands of Iwo Jima.*"

I put my helmet on, to leave my hands free. It was all wet and squishy inside, but it was that kind of night. I ran bent over, like the Vietnam grunts on the Seven O'Clock News, flitting from tree to tree. My Honda was still where I'd left it, and the stereo and most of the lights were out at Myrna's. Two or three figures were lying on the living room floor, passing a joint. I could see the lighted tip glowing in the dark.

I pushed the little red Honda down the driveway. I was just reaching for the key when I was dazzled by the highbeams on Ralph's Mercedes. I was sitting directly in front of him, not twenty feet away. As casually as I could, I kick-started the Honda, snicked into gear and zipped away in the opposite direction. I could see the headlights following me, closer and closer.

It was no contest. He ran me down within a couple of blocks, pulled alongside and just edged me off the road at 60 mph. I got into the gravel along the verge, wobbled onto the grass and now totally out of control, dropped down a steep slope, sliding sideways. There was a concrete drainage ditch in the bottom, and the little Honda rolled to a stop and sort of fell over gently on its side.

I'd dropped it once on the street and torn up my ankle, and I'd fallen off a couple of times playing around in the woods out in the State Forest. Compared to that, this was nothing. I stepped off and let the Honda fall between my legs. I grabbed the ignition key, which turned the lights off, and figured it was as safe right there as anywhere. I could ride it out in the morning, but nobody was going to be able to push it out before then.

Dave found me easily, because I was still wearing my helmet with the reflective safety tape when I crawled out of the ditch on my hands and knees.

"You okay?"

"I'm beginning to feel like this isn't my night."

"It's still early."

He drove slowly down Seventeenth Street while I took off my rancid helmet and wiped some of the mud off my arms with the wet towels on the floor.

When we stopped for the light at Route 46, there were two cars ahead of us...some high-school kids coming home from a date in Dad's Buick, and in front of them, Ralph's Mercedes. I could see him and the guy in the leopard dashaiki passing a joint back and forth.

They turned East on 46, and Dave followed them. He blew by the kids in the Buick on the first straight, and came right up behind the Mercedes.

"What's that dork doing with a dumb car like that?"

"His father has bags of bucks. And it's not that dumb a car. See that chrome on the trunk, over on the right? It says six point three. That means 6.3 liters, or, let's see, yeah...386 cubic inches. It's a V-8, overhead cams, something like 300 horse. It'll do 140."

"Bullshit."

"Honest. I was with him. That thing screams. It ought to for $14,000."

"Now I know you're lying. That car cost fourteen grand?"

"Maybe more like fourteen-five."

Dave was quiet for a minute. Then heading into a gentle curve at maybe 70, he pulled up next to the Mercedes, and starting edging over towards it. Ralph looked over, recognized me, and pressed the gas. The Mercedes positively lept ahead, a lot quicker than Dave expected. He floored the throttle to get passing gear, and we were side by side again.

It was uncanny. We had a 396 Chevelle, just about the hottest Super Car in town, and we could just barely stay with this boxy blue four-door sedan with an old-fashioned grille, a stand-up hood ornament and chrome hubcaps, for Chrissake. It looked like something Richard Nixon would drive to a funeral.

After a few long sweepers, Route 46 straightened out for miles, all the way to Bean Blossom. There was no other traffic, and damn few houses until you got to the cutesy little tourist trap of Nashville, in Brown County. Dave stayed with him up to 120, at which point the Chevelle was wound out as tight as it would go. Ralph's Mercedes had us by an easy 15 mph. It pulled away until we could just barely make out the taillights, half-a-mile ahead.

"I can catch him in that curvy stretch as soon as we cross the county line."

"Uh, Dave...why? Why do we have to catch him?"

"Because he pisses me off."

"Makes sense to me."

Dave kept his foot into it as we entered the first right-hander, but he got just a foot or two wide coming out. That set him up all wrong for the left-hander. He got all sideways, scrubbing off speed, but by then it was too late. He tried the brakes, but that just made us plow straight on. We took the gutter in a bound, and disappeared into some farmer's cornfield at over 100.

I could hear the cornstalks hitting the floor under my feet like rifle shots. The headlights pointed first at the solid green wall of corn ahead of us—maybe five feet high, this time of summer—and then into the sky as we bounced over the furrows. We must have gone an eighth of a mile before the Chevelle finally sank into mud up to the axles.

Dave mowed down an arc of corn with his door,

and swatted at the mosquitos that gathered on his arms.

"Well, we may as well start walking. There's not much else to do."

"Can you find us a phone?"

"Couple miles up the road. Why?"

"I'll call Myrna to come get us."

"You really think she'll come?"

"She was laughing the last time we saw her. Besides, who else do you know that you can call at three in the morning? We can sleep over at her house."

"Well, come on then. These mosquitos haven't been fed for months."

"Just a minute. I feel a little sick."

"Not again."

I could feel it rising in the back of my throat. I couldn't help myself. I balanced my helmet on my knees and waited.

How I Spent a Lifetime in a Nash-Healey One Week

The following story is true. The names have been changed to protect the guilty...but they know who they are.

In those days, I was the barely-paid editor of a struggling magazine about antique cars, fleshing out my income by writing erotic fantasy for porno mags under an assumed name. The car magazine office was in the front half of the third floor loft where Jeanie and I lived in Manhattan...which was also the shop from which my friend George and I ran our motorcycle racing team.

I'd type all day, and work on Yamahas most of the night, testing them with 10 foot cardboard rug tubes slipped over the exhaust pipes and stuck out the window. The neighbors only complained if we revved up the two-stroke Yamahas after 3 am, and the only time Jeanie got *really* fed up about living in a combination office/motorcycle shop was one night when George spray-painted his gas tank metalflake blue in the middle of her all-white living room.

We were just about out of money, and then I sold a couple of ideas for children's books to a New York publisher. Part of the deal was that the publisher would pay my expenses to spend two weeks in California taking pictures of motorcycles. They'd be used to illustrate one of the books.

Even before I flew to Los Angeles, I had this idea of buying an old car in California—I was thinking of a '40 Ford—and driving it across the country. That would give me something to write about for the first of a series of articles about living every day with an old car, and I could bill my travel expenses to the magazine and pocket the return airfare.

I borrowed a car in Los Angeles from one of the PR offices—I remember it as an especially homely, yellow Mazda RX-2—and dutifully sped around Los Angeles taking motorcycle photos. I was on my way up Santa Monica Boulevard one afternoon to meet a Norton owner in Malibu, when I noticed a used car lot.

Half of it was run-of-the-mill Chevies and Fords from the Sixties, sadly decorated with plastic pennants and hand-lettered signs. The other half was filled with rows of old Fords—'40 Fords—Cadillacs and miscellaneous old crocks. Within seconds, I was poking around, opening doors and inhaling that wonderful aroma—part mildew, part damp wool, part burned oil—that says Old Car.

Way over in the back, against the chain-link fence, was an ancient sports car even I didn't recognize. It had the oval grille and hood scoop from a Nash Ambassador, but the body was seamless aluminum, shaped kind of like a gigantic MGA. The windshield was made up of two flat panes, set into a handmade aluminum frame. It had a huge padded leatherette top, what was called a Carson Top back in the Forties, and a single bench seat upholstered in matching white vinyl with blue piping that once had matched the faded blue metallic paint on the body.

I opened the hood. The engine was a Nash Ambassador Six, but someone had built an intake manifold out of an old piece of exhaust tubing, and bolted on two British SU carburetors. Just about the time I was starting to walk away, a guy who could only be a used car salesman—he was wearing a brown and yellow windowpane suit and a bad toupee—steered me back with an arm around my shoulders.

"What is this thing?" I said.

"It's called a Nash-Healey...1951. Built in England by Donald Healey. You know, Austin-Healeys? The same guy."

"But it has a Nash engine."

"It has a Nash gearbox, too. Three-speed with overdrive. The chassis is from something called a Healey Silverstone. That ugly top isn't right, of course."

"Is this the only one?"

"It's the only one I've ever seen. But I've got a book in the office that says they built about a hundred of 'em. You wanna see the book?"

He had me, and he knew it. The book was a Floyd Clymer hardcover that was so old even back then that the pages had all turned yellow around the edges. But everything he'd told me was true, at least according to Clymer. For what I had in mind, the thing was perfect. An exotic sports car, but with an American engine. Not just an American engine, but a *Nash*, of all things. That would please my fanatical readers. I never thought about '40 Fords again.

We bargained our way down to $2200 including a tune-up and a new battery, to be ready the next week. Jeanie cabled me the money, just about the last of our savings, and the insurance agent who covered my Norton Commando street bike wrote up a policy for a Nash-Healey over the phone. I got California license plates, and on a Monday afternoon in late August, I dropped the Mazda off in Compton and took a cab up to Santa Monica.

The whole five-man sales staff and the lone mechanic turned out to wave goodbye, only smirking when they thought I wasn't looking. I stowed my camera case, film bag and suitcase in the surprisingly large trunk, got a set of quick instructions on how to use the overdrive and headed off for the Santa Monica Freeway that would take me to Interstate 15 and Las Vegas.

By the time I got out of there, it was after five, and so I hit downtown LA in rush hour. It was nearly eight in the evening by the time I started up the long grade to Victorville. By then I had gotten used to the Nash-Healey, and was enjoying myself more with every mile. The thing actually handled pretty well up until about 80 mph, and it would cruise comfortably at 70 mph in Overdrive.

The drill was to run up through the 3-speed column-shift Nash transmission, then depress the clutch, pause 1...2...3...then pull the big white knob under the dash. There'd be a distinct clunk, at which point you could then release the clutch and get back on the gas at dramatically-reduced revs. That old Nash Six had so much torque that it would pull the long desert grades in Overdrive, where other cars were shifting down once, or even twice.

I stopped in Barstow in the dark, to top up the gas tank and radiator, add a quart of oil and generally check things over. The odometer read a little over 40,000, and there was no reason not to believe it. The car was twenty years old, but there was nothing wrong with it that a good weekend of scrubbing wouldn't solve.

From the very beginning, I never considered the fact that I might not be able to drive virtually non-stop from Los Angeles to New York in an antique sports car. The Nash felt like it would just keep going and going, loping along at 70 mph as long as I could hold the huge white plastic wheel and keep my foot on the gas.

I hit Las Vegas around 2 am, and spent the remainder of the night in a cheap motel at the very end of The Strip. It took me all the next day to make Richfield, Utah where I could join up with Interstate 70 heading towards Denver. I ate a quick dinner, and when I came out at dusk, the thermometer on the restaurant wall was still reading over 100 degrees. The kid in the dusty service station looked over the Nash-Healey dubiously.

"You have any trouble today?"

"Nope. Only overheated twice. Otherwise, it ran like a clock."

"You want some advice, Mister...you're gonna be climbing all the way from here to Denver. Lotsa folks get car trouble in the desert."

"What should I do?"

"If I were you, I'd drive all night...it'll be a lot cooler. You'll be in Denver tomorrow morning."

I stocked up on bottled water, fruit and candy bars, napped for an hour on the wide bench seat, and started out again in the dark. The temperature dropped to maybe 80, and stayed there. But that was a lot cooler than it had been during the day.

There were places out there where you could look for 50 miles in every direction...and not see a single light. I'd never been so alone, so far from other people. All night I motored through the darkness, more alone than I've ever been, before or since. I stopped a couple times for gas, and there were some stretches of I-70 that were under construction, but for the most part it was as easy a drive as it could be.

According to the account I copied out of Clymer's book, Donald Healey had built Nash-Healeys for LeMans every year in the early Fifties. One year they finished Third overall behind a pair of Mercedes 300SLs, another year they were Fourth, another year Sixth. I thought about this a lot as I drove on through the night.

I was doing twenty-four hours straight in a Nash-Healey, cruising at 70 mph. Duncan Hamilton, Tony Rolt and the other British Nash-Healey racers averaged over 90 mph for twenty-four hours at LeMans, hitting 140 mph down Mulsanne. As Winston Churchill might have put it, "They were a tough and hardy lot. They did not journey all this way, because they were made of sugar candy." It's amazing what quotes your memory can dredge up at 4 am.

The high-point of my trip was coming into the Rockies at dawn. After two days in the desert, there were trees, real pine trees, dark green and shiny, next to a stream cascading over rocks with a spray of white foam that was absolutely dazzling after driving in the dark all night. I crawled through Vail in the morning traffic jam, crossed the divide and came down into Denver before noon.

Like millions of other travelers, I found Denver disappointing...a dirty, midwest industrial city an hour from the mountains. Hardly the Rockie Mountain High I expected. I slept all day and night, and the next morning, refreshed and happy to be leaving Denver, I headed for Kansas City. All day I stared at corn fields, more corn than I could imagine anyone ever wanting or needing, corn by the square mile, by the hundreds of square miles, all of it ripening in the late summer sun.

It took me until after midnight to get to Columbia, Missouri where I'd miss the Kansas City rush hour in the morning. For the first time, I was tired and bored. The Healey had no radio, so I sang, I talked to myself...anything to stay awake. My right knee started to throb from pushing against the Healey's strong throttle return springs, and I started driving with my left foot wedged on the pedal, my right leg tucked under me on the seat.

Next day, Kansas City to Indianapolis. Now the predominant color was British Racing Green, in sharp contrast to the dusty tan of the Far West and the delicate corn green of Kansas. The Healey still ran without missing a beat, averaging 23 mpg at 70 mph. It even had a pretty good ride, because of—or in spite of—weird cast-alloy trailing arms which held the front wheels approximately in position.

Of course, it got lots of attention from other drivers. At almost every gas stop, there would be somebody to tell me about the Nash they used to own...didn't look anything like this, though, Sonny. Outside St. Louis, I remember there was one old guy who not only knew all about the Nash-Healey, but had owned one back when they were new.

"Damn thing was strong as a tank," he said. "Except for that aluminum body. Used to leave a dent every time a bird shit on it."

The last day, I did Indianapolis to New York City. I went to graduate school in Bloomington, Indiana, so that was a drive I'd done a dozen times before. The worst part was winding through the Pennsylvania mountains, and even here, the Nash would roll along in Overdrive, no problem. Somewhere in Ohio, a small gas leak started around one SU, but not enough to worry about.

I finally pulled into Manhattan around 3 am Sunday morning. It was so late, none of the parking garages were still open, so I left the car in the parking lot at Bellevue Hospital...open all night...and limped home with my luggage. I had already arranged by phone with a friend of mine to store the car in his garage up in Westchester, so it wouldn't be in Manhattan.

Around noon on Sunday, Jeanie and I walked over and got the Nash-Healey out of the lot to drive it to Rye while there was no traffic. I accelerated slowly away from the traffic light on Third Avenue at 34th Street, heading for a gas station a couple of blocks further north. There was no other traffic; I was in the middle of four empty lanes heading North.

At the same time as I leisurely accelerated away from the light, a fellow named Francisco Francesco, driving a '69 Pontiac GTO, fish-tailed away from the light one block behind me. By the time Francisco caught up with me, the Nash-Healey was doing about 10 mph, the GTO was over 60 mph. For some reason, instead of passing me on the left, he decided to pass on the right.

He misjudged by about a foot. With a thunderclap that swiveled heads for blocks around, his GTO peeled my Nash-Healey like a grape. When I spun to a stop in the center of the intersection, Jeanie simply stepped out through the hole where the side of the car used to be and ran to the curb. From front to rear, the Healey's aluminum body had been neatly sliced open, revealing the chassis and interior like a technical cutaway.

Francisco's Pontiac ended up against the curb half a block away, with minor dents around the left front fender. The young Irish cop who answered the accident call went over and pulled a grapefruit-sized ball of aluminum out of Francisco's left headlight. This grapefruit had a windwing attached to one side...it used to be my passenger door.

Francisco had no insurance, but he found a friendly agent to back-date a policy for him. Friends of mine who owned a parking garage agreed to temporarily store the Healey until I could borrow a trailer and bring it someplace else to get it repaired. I called the only restorer in New York with any experience working with aluminum. He quoted me $15,000 to repair the Healey's body...in other words, he really didn't want to touch it.

I borrowed a car and a trailer from my friend Jerry, who raced Pintos, and Ed Jurist at the Vintage Car Store in Nyack reluctantly let me store the wreck in the parking lot behind his building. I wrote an editorial in my magazine, ending with an appeal for another Nash-Healey body. By the time the article came out, Francisco's insurance company had paid me $2200.

A couple of readers called to tell me about another Nash-Healey—this one with a perfect body but a rusted-out chassis—not more than thirty miles from where my wreck was sitting. I borrowed Jerry's trailer and tow-car again, drove up there and bought the hulk for $700. Uncle Ed was not exactly thrilled when I deposited a second junk Nash-Healey in his lot, and he made me cover the two of them with a big blue tarp so as not to insult the Bentley Continental Flying Spur parked on one side and the Bugatti Type 13 on the other.

And there they sat...for over a year. I took some of the insurance money and built a Yamaha for the AMA races at Daytona in March...and spent the rest for another Yamaha engine after I'd blown that one up at 140 mph on the Daytona banking. After months of subtle hints that I ignored, Uncle Ed finally told me point blank I'd have to find another place to store the two Healeys...they were driving away customers. Jeanie and I were still living in Manhattan, and there was no way I could put two Nash-Healeys in a third-floor walkup, like I could the Yamahas.

One day, out of the blue, the phone rang in my office. The voice on the other end belonged to an old car enthusiast from Maryland. He collected Nash-Healeys—he had something like thirty-eight of the things—and he was ready to buy my two sight unseen. I told him they both were junk, and sent him a roll of pictures. No matter. He planned to corner the market in Nash-Healeys and open a museum.

He cheerfully agreed to pay me $1900 for the two wrecks, which put me $1200 ahead for my total Nash-Healey ownership.

True to his word, the Maryland collector met me at Uncle Ed's one afternoon, loaded the two wrecks onto a trailer, smilingly paid me cash in hundred dollar bills and drove away out of my life. Years later, a friend actually visited this guy's collection, and there were, as promised, Nash-Healeys by the dozen. My two were in the same condition they were the day he bought them, still forlornly snuggled together under their blue plastic cover. For all I know, they're still there.

My right knee bothers me sometimes after a long drive, sort of a dull ache that starts under the kneecap and lasts for a day or two. And now I remember why. It's the only legacy I have from that week I spent all alone, fighting the too-stiff return springs on a pair of leaky SUs that Donald Healey had bolted onto the side of a Nash engine. It seemed like a good idea at the time.

Black Hearts in the Bronx

Luv always likes to start the races himself. He crouches in the space between the front fenders, left arm in the air. Tonight, Brooklyn Slows is on the left in his 454 Corvette; Fast John is on the right in his Traco-engined 427 Camaro. When Luv lowers his arm to horizontal, they pop ‘em into gear and wind ‘em up to redline. Then like a cat, Luv springs straight up in the air, madly waving the red bandana that is his trademark. He sidesteps the fishtailing slicks as they blast by him, the sound of their open exhausts rattling off the boarded-up brownstones on either side of 208th Street.

When they pass the Black Hearts clubhouse five blocks away, the Corvette's brake lights blink on, and one of Luv's lieutenants, stationed on that side of the street, waves a white bandana signifying the car in his lane has won. Fast John never touches his brakes. The Camaro hits a raised manhole cover as he crosses the intersection, veers sharply to the right, catches the curb broadside and rolls viciously onto its roof before sliding into an iron railing. It finally comes to rest, upside down, on the immovable brown sandstone steps of an abandoned Victorian row house. It bursts into flames just after Fast John crawls from the wreck. He makes it all the way to the opposite sidewalk before passing out on his stomach.

By now, the gamblers are already lining up, bobbing and jostling, to collect their winnings from Jambo, the treasurer of the Black Hearts. Jambo is Swahili for "hi, how ya doin'" and his gang name is a typical example of ironic New York humor. Jambo is an unsmiling, cold-eyed bastard with a heart-etched gold tooth, whose only pleasure comes from stuffing hundred dollar bills into the cash box his assistant carries at all times. When he walks down the sidewalk followed by his retainers, men switch to the other side of the street and women move back off the stoop.

People in the neighborhood say, "Jambo? Only heart that man got be the one on his tooth."

Jambo works for Luv, the president of the Black Hearts. This is a position to which Luv has elected himself by slashing anybody who disagrees with him. He wears a red bandana tied around his shaved head, one gold heart-shaped earring, a denim jacket with the arms cut off and a heart shape worked in rhinestone studs on the back, jeans, engineer boots and a 6 inch bone-handled hunting knife in a scabbard stuck in the top of his right boot. As a kid, he carved H A T E into the knuckles of his right hand, and L U V into the knuckles of his left. People had stopped trying to teach him to spell pretty early on.

Three or four of Luv's members pick up Fast

John and carry him into their clubhouse. By the time I walk up there, he is sitting up on the couch in the front of the former fruit market, looking out the window at the still burning wreck of all his worldly possessions and weakly shaking his head. Fast John is this skinny white kid from Long Island with a Jesus Freak haircut, a yellow headband and bad skin. He lives at home to save money and pours every cent he makes as a nightclub DJ into his '68 Camaro, the one that is now merrily burning half a block away.

Fast John and I are sitting on a couch on 208th Street at 3:00 am, watching everything he owns burn to a crisp because of Brooklyn Slows. Brooklyn Slows is a local legend around the New York area. He is *old*, probably thirty-five, pudgy and out of shape. He is an albino with delicate, translucent skin, never seen outside of his Uncle Joe Corelli's Bar and Grill until well after dark.

He has white, shoulder-length hair, blue-tinted glasses and a dark blue satin Yankees warm-up jacket with "Lenny" embroidered over the pocket. Brooklyn Slows' real name is Leonard...but everybody, even his mother, calls him Slows to his face and The Slow Man when referring to him in the third person.

This is because as a child, Leonard was such a poor student, his Uncle Joe said to his mother, "Ya know, Yvonne, I think dat kid of yours got a real bad case of da slows." You can go into any Italian restaurant, fast food joint or biker bar between Englishtown and Riverhead and people know about The Slow Man.

What Brooklyn Slows has going for him are a

complete lack of scruples, fearlessness and reflexes so good he can sit at his table in Corelli's and pick flies out of the air between his thumb and forefinger. When Slows leaves the place, there is always a pile of dead flies on the red and white checkered tablecloth, next to his half-eaten plate of calimari.

He has been street racing for close to twenty years. At first he was just a strange, overweight teenage kid looking for something to do, because none of the girls would go out with him. But he turned out to be a *natural*...he plumped his broad bottom into a race car, and it went faster than it ever had before. Pretty soon, he was a hired driver on the late-night, permanent floating street racing circuit that ran Northern Boulevard on Wednesday night, the lower end of the abandoned West Side Highway on Friday night and Luv's 208th Street turf on Saturday night.

This is money racing, you understand. Slows will no longer even bother to show up unless the bet is at least five big ones, cash showing, deposited by both parties into Jambo's greedy but surprisingly trustworthy hands. The Black Hearts take ten percent for "expenses," and the winner collects the rest.

For the past year, Slows has been racing a Corvette professionally built and maintained for him by a race shop in Mineola. It is almost a tube chassis funny car, with a blown 454 Chevy rat motor. What challenges even The Slow Man's incredible reflexes is the Corvette's stock wheelbase. The car will rear back and ride the bumper all the way through a pass, if he lets it. The highpoint of his career was the night he spotted Jersey Jerry's Hemi Challenger two car lengths and still beat him for $15,000.

When the wreck of the Camaro has cooled, Fast John and I look around for anything salvagable, find nothing, and walk away. I drive him home to Hempstead, and just have time to shower and shave before leaving for my office in Manhattan. I don't hear from John for a week, and then he calls me late at night, after the club where he works has closed. He has borrowed a car trailer from our mutual buddy Joel the Flame, and he wants me to go scouting. If he wants to go scouting, this means that Fast John has decided to build another race car to challenge The Slow Man.

Cars are always being abandoned in New York. Some nice work-a-hubby will be commuting from Greenwich in his Buick, and he'll run out of gas on the West Side Highway. "Damn it," he'll say to himself. "That's the last time I let that brat Roger borrow my car for a date." After vainly waiting an hour for a policeman to stop and help him, work-a-hubby hikes down the verge to the next exit and buys gas at the nearest station, after leaving a $50 deposit for a $5 gas can.

When he finally gets back, his Buick is still there, all right. But the wheels have been jerked off and the car allowed to settle on its axles. The passenger window is broken and the radio is gone. Work-a-hubby drops his gas can, realizes his briefcase had been in the front seat, walks back to the gas station and calls his insurance man. Within a day, the Buick will be picked as clean as a Thanksgiving turkey, leaving just a shell that's of no use to anybody...except somebody scouting for a free carcass out of which to build a race car.

Fast John and I find pretty slim pickings. He

finally settles on an almost new Nissan 300ZX, complete except for the wheels and engine, that has been recently parked in a break-down lane on the Long Island Expressway. The windows haven't even been broken yet. We drag it onto the trailer, and bring it back to his parent's garage. We strip all the numbers off that we can find, then strip the paint, just in case.

Over the next two months, we build a new car according to the unwritten rules and peculiar conditions of our race circuit. The trunk floor comes out, to be replaced by two huge aluminum wheel tubs. A friend of John's welds up a rollcage/tubular chassis that is much heavier than drag racers normally use. Rather than lightened, the suspension is beefed up by welding steel angle reinforcements onto everything, to deal with the potholed New York streets on which we race. A local SCCA type who lives near John's parents helps us figure out stiff sway bars and shocks, rather than the usual drag racing floppy shocks. We have to sacrifice weight transfer for road holding...*rough* road holding.

John buys a narrowed Summers rear end with a locker differential and 6.56 gears. I strip the whole interior, then according to the peculiar custom of New York street racers, replace every panel with aluminum...spray painted with black texture paint to look like vinyl. We put in a pair of fiberglass road racing seats with harnesses, and a full set of SW gauges in an aluminum panel that stretches all the way across the dash. The Cragar alloy wheels and 17 inch wide M&H slicks come straight off another friend's wrecked funny car, along with narrow Cragars and Goodyear Frontrunners for the front.

The 440 cubic inch Wedge was originally in a

Super Stock Barracuda. It is a loaner from Jersey Jerry, who'd help anybody who had a chance of beating Brooklyn Slows. He also lends us a 6-71 blower and three-hole Enderle injector, plus his beefed-up B&M Hole Shot Torqueflite and Trans Go. We put a scoop on the hood to clear the supercharger and injector, with a screen that prevents you from looking inside. We also install locking hood pins to keep anyone from checking things out too closely. Once we spray the body with light grey primer and replace the chrome bumpers, it looks just like any other clapped-out 300ZX.

It is September before Fast John puts the word on the street that he is after Brooklyn Slows to the tune of $10,000, straight up. Part of the front money is his, part is mine. In another week the word comes back. The Slow Man will accept John's challenge, but only if the stakes double to $20,000. Take it or leave it, this Saturday night, Hearts clubhouse, straight up, 2:00 am, Jambo holds the pot. If we aren't there by 2:30, the word will be out and Fast John will never get another race in New York. Jersey Jerry comes through for the other ten grand.

"You want dis Slows guy. I want dis Slows guy. How much ya need?"

Luv is playing the expansive host when we arrive at 2:00 am on a cold, windy night. A $40,000 grudge match is the biggest race the Hearts have ever staged, which adds to their prestige...plus substantially to their treasury. For which Jambo is especially happy. There are a couple of new cops in the neighborhood, who are trying to shake them down for an additional grand a week.

We stand around on the dark street, smoking

unfiltered Chesterfields, talking, scuffling our feet and taking sideways glances at the car. Luv has stationed gang members at both sides of every intersection to control traffic. Jambo is busy making book with a couple of dozen spectators...hundred dollar minimum, 3 to 1 on The Slow Man, 9 to 2 on Fast John. The punters know Brooklyn Slows and his Corvette, but the Nissan is new, foreign and different. Besides which, the last time they'd seen Fast John, he was face down in the street next to a burning wreck. His odds go to 10 to 1. At that point, I can recoup my losses. I put my last thousand dollars on Fast John.

At 2:30 exactly, Brooklyn Slows arrives with his old Chrysler tow car, pulling the Corvette on an open trailer. Behind him is a blue and white New York City police cruiser, strobe lights flashing bleakly. The Slow Man ignores his escort and quickly unloads the Corvette next to Fast John's 300ZX.

The two cops get out and start towards the race cars. Luv intercepts them in the middle of the street. There is some earnest conversation, Luv waves his arm in the general direction of the fifty gang members stationed at the intersections and along the sidewalks, a gang that is effectively the only law and order for a ten block area of the Bronx. There is more conversation. Then the policemen turn and walk back towards their car, just as Slows splashes a bucket full of bleach in front of them, preparatory to running his burnout. They sidestep the puddle with dark looks, and go back to lean against their cruiser.

Luv comes over to Fast John. "You be ready?"

John hands over twenty thousand dollar bills, which Luv passes to Jambo for safe-keeping.

"What they want?"

"They want trouble."

"Waddya say?"

"I say, 'Da Man don't mess wid me, I don't mess wid da Man.'"

"Look," says The Slow Man, handing his cash directly to Jambo. "Youse guys come here to fuck around with cops, or you come to race?"

The drivers belt themselves into their cars, Fast John looking pale and nervous, Slows looking like the Pillsbury dough boy hyped on speed balls. When they start up, the sound is incredible, a physical blow that bounces off the brownstones and hammers you in the chest. The boom of the open exhausts seems to synchronize with your heartbeat...*wumba, WUMBA, wumba, WUMBA*. People appear on the front stoops of the houses that are still occupied, grinning, hands over their ears. It is a point of honor that the Hearts take no notice of the noise, as the beat batters them deaf.

Fast John and Slows do side-by-side bleach burnouts, then pull up to where Luv is standing in the middle of 208th Street, left arm raised in the air, the strobes from the police cruiser like lasers shooting off the rhinestones on his jacket. The cars nuzzle up to his hips, as he dramatically keeps his back to them, waiting patiently for the two drivers to jockey themselves into line. When they are done, the arm comes down to horizontal, then Luv disappears from view between the fenders.

Fast John is already launching when Luv springs into the air, waving his bandana. Being in the right lane gives John a split second head start, because he can see Luv's legs tense to jump. To

Slows, Luv is completely obscured until he leaps, and it is a point of honor that The Slow Man has never redlighted. He has never needed to.

The Corvette shudders into motion, front wheels a foot in the air, chassis twisting from the torque, and catches up with the little Nissan in the first hundred yards. After that, who can tell? From where we stand, two dull gray shadows hurl themselves down the narrow corridor of a city street. Five uptown blocks equal a quarter-mile, at which point we can't even see them in the darkness. We can hear that neither one lifted, and we can see the white bandanas come up. And then we see brake lights.

Fast John and Slows leave the cars where they stopped, and walk back side-by-side to get their tow rigs. The two finish line bandana-wavers come with them, along with a growing crowd of Black Hearts, gamblers and neighbors.

"Who won?"

"Don't nobody rightly know. He say he won. *He* say *he* won. We say they be tied when they pass us. Don't nobody rightly know."

Luv turns to Slows. "You wanna run again?"

"Not tonight."

"We got no winner, we got no profit. Jambo, here's what we do. The Black Hearts take an extra ten percent for our trouble, we give you back what's left. We return all the bets, square."

"But that's $8000 you took tonight from me and Slows."

Luv reaches down to his boot, and comes up with Fast John's shirt front in one hand, his hunting knife in the other. He lays the knife point alongside John's neck.

"You got some problem with that, white boy?"

Fast John shakes himself free and turns to Brooklyn Slows. "Okay, Slow Man. Next Saturday, same time, same place. Straight up, fifteen grand says I whip your fat ass."

The Slow Man nods, once, and turns away towards his tow car, wincing as the police strobes catch him in the eyes, bringing pain through the blue glass. He'll be there. Hasn't he always been there? Anytime, kid. Anytime.

The Green Dragon

"Remember Barney Oldfield?" rasped the old man. "You're darn tootin'." He paused to cough and spit delicately into his handkerchief. "He were a piss-cutter, he were. Oldfield would smoke your ten cent ceegars, steal your money and screw your wife, and smile while he did it. But he were the best race driver I ever seen, and I seen 'em all. A drivin' fool, that man were.

"I can remember it better'n yesterday, the first time I met up with Oldfield. It musta been the summer of nineteen-four, cause I had my first long pants that summer, and I got them when I went to work for my father at the Peerless race shop. Yep, musta been nineteen-four...

We was living in Cleveland then, in a third-story walkup off Euclid Avenue out near University Heights. Pop were working for Peerless; he'd ride his bicycle—Peerless, of course—all the way over to the factory on Lisbon Street, six mornings a week.

Pop came home one night in June, swung my

mother around in the kitchen, and said, "Got a kiss, Muriel, for the new head of the Peerless racing department?"

My mother, always practical, gave him a peck on the cheek and went back to peeling potatoes. "Didn't know you had a racing department."

"We do now. And I'm it. And I got a raise to forty dollars a week."

"Why Clarence, we'll be rich." This time she gave 'em a proper kiss, right there in the kitchen with me watchin', sitting at the old oak table doing my homework.

"And Junior, here, is gonna be my assistant, aren't ya, Speedie. Mr. Mooers said I can hire you for the summer, soon as school's over. How's a dollar a day sound?"

Well, that sounded all right to me. Assistant to the head of the Peerless racing department! I musta grinned pretty wide, because Pop came over and punched me in the arm. "Golly Jeepers," I shouted.

There were a confident knock on the rusty screen door. Pop opened it and drew in a small man, not much bigger than me, with a broad forehead, dark hair parted in the middle and a striped four-button suit that musta cost him fifty dollars. He were chewin' on an unlit cigar and holding one of those soft tweed golf caps we wore back then.

"Muriel," Pop said proudly, "this here's Berna Eli Oldfield. He's our new racing driver. We're gonna be seeing a lot of each other this summer."

"I hope that extends to you, too, Mrs. Wesson," said Oldfield, smiling. He produced a bunch of flowers from behind his back, like a magician conjuring up a trick. "These are for you. Hope you like roses."

My mother's face turned as pink as the flowers. She dropped the spoon she was holding and put her fingers to her cheek. They left a little trail of flour. "Oh, Clarence, how could you bring a guest home without telling me? Speedie, clean your books off the table."

Oldfield reached into his pocket and produced a small cardboard box. "Glad to meet you, Speedie," he said. "This is for you."

It were a stamped tin model of the Winton Bullet, Oldfield's race car that held the world's record.

"Golly, Mr. Oldfield. Wait'll I show the guys at school."

Barney Oldfield were already a pretty big noise when he took us all out to dinner that warm night, driving downtown in the Winton tourer they'd give him. Alexander Winton had hired him as a professional driver to race the Winton Bullet at horse tracks all over the country, after Oldfield had beat him driving Henry Ford's 999. Now Oldfield were fired by Winton and come to drive for Peerless.

Only thing were, Peerless didn't have a real race car, only one cut-down Model Twelve passenger car that Pop's boss, chief engineer Louis Mooers, had crashed at the Irish Gordon Bennett races the year before. Joe Tracy had took the rebuilt Peerless to Daytona Beach in the winter, and run eighty miles an hour. That were pretty good, almost the land speed record in those days. But that damned Peerless handled so awful, Tracy wanted no more part of it.

Mr. Mooers had built a test track, a real banked oval but only a quarter-mile around, right on the roof of the Peerless factory. First thing he done, Oldfield took that old race car up on the roof to "see what she'll do, Speedie." What she'd do was overheat thanks to a crazy surface radiator Mooers had designed out of copper tubing. So Pop took off the copper tubes and made a real radiator that sat up front between the frame rails.

Pop and I also took off most of the bodywork, threw away the passenger seat, bolted the driver's bucket seat right down on top of the frame rails and lowered the steering column so Oldfield had to bend over like a jockey to drive. Then we covered the wood spoke road wheels with big discs of aluminum, inside and out. When we was done, Oldfield had us paint the whole damn thing bright green.

Oldfield were a showman, you gotta give 'em that. "Clarence," he said, pointin' with his ceegar, "ain't nobody gonna forget they seen that green automobile." About a week later, Oldfield showed up with a leather racing outfit—pants, coat and golf cap—dyed a bright green to match. I thought that were the sharpest outfit I'd ever seen. I went on about it so much, Oldfield finally got matching green caps for Pop and me. "Team uniform," he said with a laugh. He sold his Winton tourer, and Peerless gave him a new Model Eleven roadster to drive. Oldfield had that painted bright green, too.

Almost every evening that July, Oldfield would come by the race shop where Pop and me was working on the car, poke around a while, then drive us home in his new green roadster, me sitting tall in the mother-in-law seat bolted on the rear. Pretty soon, my mother got in the habit of having a pitcher of lemon squash ready for us men, with a cold supper for later on. She seemed to suddenly have new silk skirts and fancy lace waists to wear, and her heavy auburn hair were piled pretty up on her head and tied with a big white bow.

She and I would listen quietly while Pop and Oldfield tried to figure out more ways to make the big green car faster or more reliable. We all three of us hung on Oldfield's every word, and we would solemnly shake his hand goodnight when he left. Pop even started smoking ceegars. "We're a team, Speedie," he said. "Gonna be the best race team in the world."

It musta been about the first week in August, Pop sent me over to Will Murphy's Machine Shop to pick up some steel rod so he could make a brace for the cowl. On the way back, I rode my bike through Metropolitan Park to get some cool air. Parked right out next to the lake were that bright green roadster of Oldfield's. You couldn't mistake it.

"So this are where he spends his days while Pop and me is workin' on that race car," I said to myself. "I'll just go over and see if he needs any errands run, or anything." I never got off my bike, for at that minute Oldfield came walking from around the bend.

His coat, collar and tie was all off, and he had one arm around the waist of a thin woman in a pretty white linen suit whose heavy auburn hair had obviously come down and been pinned back up in a hurry. She were carrying the white hair bow she always wore. I didn't wait around for them to spot me, but pedalled it as fast as I could go back to the race shop.

"Whatsamatter, Speedie? Your face is all red."

"Nuthin', Pop. Musta got somethin' in my eye."

Oldfield's first race for Peerless were the middle of August, nineteen-four, at a horse track outside St. Louis. Racing back then weren't all organized with rules and stuff like it is now. There weren't no automobile race courses, and there weren't more 'n a dozen race cars in the whole United States of America.

Instead, some damned promoter'd stage a grudge match between two or three cars at a local horse track. If nobody else showed up, one car would circle around as an exhibition and try to break some hoked up speed record. The horse track at St. Louis were a pip. It was right in Fairgrounds Park, almost downtown, lined with new-painted white fences inside and out and paved with clay smoothed out by horse-drawn drags. There was even some big wooden grandstands set up along the straights.

We stayed in the Union Hotel, with electric lights and indoor plumbing and feather pillows on the beds. Pop weren't gonna let me come, at first, but Oldfield got Mr. Mooers to pay for not only me, but my mother, too.

"Muriel deserves a holiday, Clarence," he said. "And if you won't give 'er one, I will." And so my mother came along to keep Oldfield company during the hot summer days, driving around St. Louis in his fancy Peerless roadster, wearing her white linen suit and a big white flowered hat with a veil. Meantimes, Pop and me was working, always working, on that damn green car.

There musta been five thousand people around that horse track on Saturday afternoon when we come in. Pop was steerin' the green car with me standing next to him, being pulled by a two-horse team. Oldfield and my mother followed in the roadster, along with the promoter, a sharp-faced feller in a checked suit named Will Pickens. I hated Pickens on sight.

After a lot of hot air and hullabaloo from Pickens, Oldfield came struttin' out in his green leather outfit, wearing a pair of glass goggles, a new ten cent ceegar between his teeth.

"You know me," he yelled. "Barney Oldfield."

They gave him a big cheer as Pop and me pushed the Peerless to get her started, while Oldfield waved to the crowd. Pickens had a big ship's chronometer, and he made a show of setting it up to time Oldfield around the one-mile track.

Then he called, real formal, "Are ye ready, Mr. Oldfield?" and fired off a pistol. He needn't have bothered. Barney did one lap to get everythin' warmed up and raised such a cloud a dust nobody could see nothing. He came blind down the front straight into his own dust, pitched 'er sideways where he thought the corner must be and went right through that damn white fence and into a pair of farm wagons parked there full of spectators.

Accordin' to the St. Louis *Post-Dispatch*, the dead folks was a pair of cousins from downstate Missouri named Claude and Eustace Barrington. Oldfield broke up his ribs pretty bad and holed a lung, and when my mother saw him all covered with blood, she fainted dead away and had to be revived with smellin' salts and brandy. There weren't anything cost more than a nickel worth savin' off that evil old Peerless and Pop sold her on the spot for scrap.

Oldfield stayed in the St. Louis hospital for a month. My mother didn't want to leave him there alone with strangers, but Pop finally convinced her we had to get back to Cleveland. Mr. Mooers told Pop it was a "golden opportunity" to build Oldfield a better racing car, and we'd better get going right now because Will Pickens had already booked twenty different races in September and October all over the country. Oldfield's crash had made him even more famous.

Pop were chock full of ideas on how to make the new car handle better. "We gotta get the weight down low, Speedie," he said, "and more in the center between the wheels." He took a standard Peerless passenger car frame and turned it upside down. The axles were now above the frame rails, sitting on leaf springs, so the whole chassis was maybe a foot closer to the ground than it had been five minutes before.

Me and Pop moved that great seventeen-liter lump of an engine back in the center of the upside down frame, with the driver's seat behind it on the left so Oldfield could see the inside of the lefthand corners coming up on a horse track. Oldfield would sit hunched over the wheel in a padded leather bucket seat, with his left foot caught in a little stirrup on the outside of the frame.

Up front, Pop built a tall radiator out of brass tubing, pointed in the middle to "split the wind." When we was done, we painted everything "Oldfield Green." That slippery promoter Will Pickens come by one day and looked at this big green car with the dozens of shiny brass radiator tubes. "Why that damn thing looks just like a big green dragon," he said. And he had Pop paint "Green Dragon" in big letters on the sides of the frame. “I can sell the hell outa that, Sport. The Peerless Green Dragon.”

Oldfield showed up at our apartment one night the beginning of September, just in time for supper, bold as brass. “Clarence, Muriel...I wancha to meet my new wife, Grace. She was my nurse in that hospital in St. Louis. That I'm standin' here before you tonight the happiest man in the world, is entirely due to her.” The loud crash behind me were my mother fainting with a platter of hot cornbread in her hand.

My mother weren't in such a very good mood after that, so me and Pop took to spending most of our time down to the race shop to keep outa her way. We hardly ever saw Oldfield and his missus except at the races, and then we was all too busy to talk much. Seems like Pop didn't have much to say to Oldfield, anyway, no more, and that pretty little nurse from St. Louis mostly kept to herself, at least where we was concerned.

“You know me...Barney Oldfield” raced at twenty different tracks that fall and won sixteen races. Course, there weren't never no more'n one or two other cars, but he beat ‘em all. And seems like everywhere we went, Oldfield and the Peerless Green Dragon set a new American speed record. Course, Oldfield's buddy Pickens were readin' the “official” stopwatch, and sometimes he would even have hired the “competition” so Oldfield could beat ‘em.

I gotta hand it to ‘em, though, Oldfield could drive. With a car that handled well, like Pop's Green Dragon, he'd just cock ‘er sideways and drift it all the way around a horse track shootin' a rooster tail of dirt ten foot high. That were some sight to see. And Pickens could get press coverage for a cat fight in an alley. By October of nineteen-four, you couldn't turn around without reading Barney Oldfield's name on everything in sight, or seeing his ugly mug grinning around a ceegar from some billboard. "You know me...Barney Oldfield."

The last race of the season were the last weekend of October at Yonkers Raceway outside New York City. Pop persuaded my mother to come along, hoping it would jolly her outa her bad mood. We took the train from Cleveland to Albany, then down the Hudson River to Yonkers. The race track musta been five miles away by horse trolley, way outside town, but it was a beaut, even fancier than St. Louis or Cleveland.

This time, Pickens had organized a ten-mile race for the "World's Championship" between Oldfield's Peerless, Leon Thery's Richard-Brasier, Maurice Bernin's Renault and Paul Sartori's Fiat. All three had more horsepower than the Green Dragon, and the French Richard-Brasier were the car that had just won the Gordon Bennett Trophy.

It didn't make no never mind to Oldfield. After ten miles, the Green Dragon were so far ahead the other three was still lost in a cloud of dust somewheres. Pickens announced a "new World's Record" of nine minutes twelve seconds for ten miles, an average of over sixty-five miles an hour. Me and Pop was so excited we couldn't talk, and both my mother and Oldfield's nurse burst into tears.

We was all standing around the dirty, greasy Green Dragon while the newspaper Johnnies made their pictures when up comes Will Pickens with the fattest man I ever seen in my life.

"This here's Mr. Blumenthal, Barney," cries Pickens. "He owns a theatre on Broadway, the Great White Way. And he's gonna put on a musical play about the Vanderbilt Cup. He's gonna build a treadmill, so you can run the Green Dragon right on the stage. Watcha think of that? The stars are you and Miss Elsie Janis, here."

Miss Elsie Janis were a peroxide blonde in a huge flowered hat, a black Astrakhan plush cape and a matching muff. I could tell she had Oldfield's attention right away. He went over to her and whispered something low that made her laugh out loud. "Why Mr. Oldfield, I believe you all tryin' take advantage a lil' ol' me."

"And," said Pickens, "Mr. Blumenthal has agreed to pay you five hundred dollars a week to appear on the stage with Miss Elsie Janis." It was quiet as a tomb, all round us.

"Why that's obscene," said a reporter near me, writing furiously in his notebook. "Why, that's more than the President makes."

"Yessir," said Oldfield, unwrapping a fresh ceegar. "But Teddy Roosevelt ain't just set a new World's Record at sixty-five miles in an hour." The crowd cheered louder than ever.

The next day when we left for Cleveland, Pickens, Oldfield and the Green Dragon stayed behind with Miss Elsie Janis. Grace decided that she really ought to visit her mother in St. Louis for a while. By the time we reached Albany, Grace and my mother had made friends, the way women do, and sitting in the waiting room in the Buffalo station, they had a good cry over Barney Oldfield, the way women do.

As for me, and Pop too, at that minute it wouldn't have made no matter to me if I ain't never seen that ceegar-eating, money-stealin', wife-screwin' son-of-a-bitch in this lifetime or the next. And I didn't neither, leastwise not for another five years. Five happiest years of my young life, back then. I gotta tell ya though, a drivin' fool, that man were. But that were another story."

Night is the Best

"You're out in forty laps." It's young Mikey shaking me from a troubled and busy sleep. "Okay?" I nod, and after an appraising look, he leaves, carefully shutting the flimsy door behind him. It is night. When I lay down, golden sunlight was glowing evenly around the curtains. Now the tiny room is alternately pitch dark and splashed with harsh artificial whiteness as the race cars charge directly at us with their driving lights. A hundred yards away, they turn abruptly left and leave me back in the soothing dark.

It is cool in the rented motorhome, and the combined hum of the generator and air-conditioner blankets the din of the cars going by at 150 mph. Paul, the Australian, is sleeping on the divan, one arm thrown over his eyes in exhaustion. Mike, from California, still dressed in his sodden driving suit, is resonantly snoring in the other narrow bunk. The whole motorhome stinks of mildew, gasoline, porta-potti disinfectant and the sweaty Nomex suits and underwear hanging from the air-conditioner, kitchen cabinets and curtain rods.

Outside is a battlefield; wet summer heat, the sound of exhausts like cannon fire, flickering lights, the stench of untreated sewage and overheated brakes, pervasive dust from the infield roads that thickens the air and settles on every surface. My driving suit, which was dry when I put it on, is soaking wet by the time I walk the quarter-mile to the pits. My shoulders and legs are stiff, my eyes gritty and puffed, I've got a blinding headache from the heat and dust, my mouth is sourly acid from too much Gatorade.

After the pitch dark paddock, our arc-lighted pit is blinding. The crew is already in position, tires on the pit apron, tools in hand. Bobby is casually hoisting the 70 lb. gas can to his shoulder with one massive hand. Rick is tensed where the front of the car will soon be, talking earnestly into his headset microphone and anxiously looking towards the dark paddock. He sees me. "He's coming in this lap. Hurry up." I take my two gallon drink bottle from the rack and fill it half and half with ice and Gatorade.

Pam, the timer who'll start her shift when I get into the car, gives me a smile. I wave her over and hand her a roll of silver duct tape off the mechanics' tool table. She tapes my radio earphones into my ears. Once I have my balaclava, helmet and glasses in place, Pam connects the earphone cord to the jack that also serves my built-in helmet microphone. She yells at me, our heads close together. "We're in fifth place overall, first in class, five laps in front of the Mitsubishi." She smiles again.

I stroll out to the pit road carrying my gloves

and ration of Gatorade, careful to keep the plastic drinking tube higher than the bottle. The crew is jumping wildly in place as Ed slews through the gravel at the end of pit road and turns sharply into the pit space. I unsnap the window net, Ed clambers stiffly out carrying his thermos, I squeeze myself in.

Drink bottle into the holder, seat adjusted, belts pulled tight until they hurt, radio plugged in, mirrors adjusted, gloves on, window net up, plastic drinking tube threaded beneath the shoulder harness, past the balaclava and into the corner of my mouth. Ed taps my leg in farewell and slams the door. The whole car tilts wildly to the side as Jim jacks up the right side to raise the fuel filler neck as high as possible.

"Radio check."

"Hi, Pam."

The car bounces back down on four new tires, new brake pads in the front, fuel spilling off the fender. Mike dilutes it with a massive bucketsplash of water. Rick is waving his arms like a semaphore.

"Go, go, go."

I accelerate out of the pits past pink-hatted stewards waving me to go faster or slower, sometimes simultaneously. The marshal at Pit Out is holding a fluorescent sign with an arrow pointing straight ahead. She circles her arm madly and I accelerate as fast as the Nissan will go.

My headache is gone, the stiffness in my muscles is gone, the icy Gatorade tastes delicious. There is only one problem; I can't see a goddamn thing.

"Pam, there's something wrong with the lights."

"Didn't Rick tell you? We lost the driving lights two hours ago. He says to find somebody to follow."

Right. Two cars overtake me going into the first corner, the effect of their combined lights absolutely dazzling. They pass me angrily on the outside, cutting close in eloquent disdain. That's better. I can follow at a distance, and now at least I can guess where the turn-in points are. Right-hander, right-hander, left-hander, brakes, down-shift, banked left-hander at full throttle, through the off-camber carrousel at the top end of Third, then Fourth, flat-out through the right-hand kink, tap the brakes before the bump, up in the air and down, hard brakes, down-shift, left-hander, hard brakes, down-shift, sharp right-hander, back up through the gears on the front straight.

"Rich, that was a 1:35." There is disappointment in her voice.

"I can't see a thing. Wait till I find somebody faster to follow."

It is like the freeway at night, only everyone is high on adrenalin and unbelievably aggressive. Familiar landmarks appear in my dim lights for an instant, then are replaced by confusing darkness. Apexes suddenly pop up, sooner by seconds than I remember. In the carrousel, I have to feel my way around, craning forward against the belts to see better. Two much faster cars stack up behind me, then viciously blast past onto the straight.

Another knot of cars going slightly faster passes me, and I make a deliberate effort to latch onto them. My rhythm is coming back. This isn't so bad. All I have to do is follow them around, using their lights. And now I'm starting to recognize my landmarks in the dark.

"31.4. Good job." There is relief in her voice.

Good, but not good enough. With a proper set of driving lights, there should be no difference between my daylight and darkness lap times. I should be turning 1:26s, but I just can't see well enough.

"Sorry I can't go faster. I just can't see on my own."

"Rick says you're doing fine. Just keep it out there through the night, and we'll race them in the morning."

The corner lights up like daylight. I go much deeper and harder, accelerating on the edge now that I can see. There are six lights spread across the hood of the car behind me, like the eyes of some iridescent insect in my mirrors. I stay in front for most of a lap, then he passes me in the dust coming out of the carrousel and rockets away down the straight, wheels hammering over the bumps. There is no way I can go that fast without a similar array of lights.

"That was a 29.4."

"The Mitsubishi just passed me. I can't run with it."

"They've put their best driver in, and he's doing 27s. Rick says don't worry about it. They're five laps behind."

"How many laps have I completed?"

"That was your twentieth lap, and you turned a 29.1. Good job."

I've caught up to Ron in the other Nissan and a Toyota, all of us circulating at roughly the same speed. The race has broken down into three clumps of traffic. There is a knot of slow cars turning 34s and 35s, the four leaders running together at 27s, then scattered duos and trios like ours running somewhere in between. Because of pit stops and accidents, the traffic mix is constantly changing.

Life has been reduced to the taillights of the cars ahead, what little I can see of the track and a black void punctuated by clouds of dust kicked up by the passing cars. There is a spectacular effect on some laps as I leave the carrousel and following traffic is coming in, their lights heading straight at me for a second. And there are the cars with driving lights at crazy angles because of accidents, illuminating the trees or the sky like searchlights.

I'm in suspension, my conscious mind a blank, the driving an automatic response to outside stimuli. It's somewhere between a runner's high and the spiritual ecstacy of Saint Theresa, a quiet peace, an inner calm achieved inside a hot, filthy race car, tires shrieking in agony at insane speeds. Only a racer could understand when Ed said yesterday, "I can't wait to get in the car. I need to relax."

"Rich, you've completed fifty laps. Halfway through your stint. You're turning consistent 29s. The Mitsubishi has slowed to 29s, as well."

After a while, you learn to recognize the pattern of lights, the headlights of the faster cars in your mirrors, the taillights of the ones that are slower. Two huge round lights, high-mounted, flanked by low oblong headlights means a Consulier GTP. Six rectangular lights is a fast-moving Mustang prototype, four round lights the race-leading Nissan. The tiny taillights of two slow-moving older Nissans and the red rectangles of the Mazdas mean I'll be held up for two or three precious seconds if I come up behind them at the wrong corner.

Four round lights in an arc appear in my

mirrors, a pattern I don't recognize. He passes me into Oak Tree and evolves into a yellow Mazda. He slices inside Ron into the carrousel, then promptly spins Big Time. Ron and I stab the brakes simultaneously, and the corner workers are treated to the sight of three cars spinning in unison. Following traffic avoids us and we set off again, having wasted twenty seconds. I pass Ron down the straight, so I'm behind the Mazda at the keyhole. He spins again, I hit the brakes, and Pam says on the radio, "Hey, it's like ballet. You're both spinning in formation right in front of me."

This time I manage to keep going and put the Mazda behind me. By the time we reach Oak Tree, his crescent of lights is back in my mirrors. I watch with uninhibited pleasure as I see them go twirling off the outside of the course in a self-inflicted cloud of dust.

"You've completed eighty laps. You ought to see a yellow fuel light any time now."

"It's already on. I forgot to tell you."

"There's a wrecker on the course."

Surprisingly, it's not the Mazda. I come into the carrousel, and there are white and yellow flags waving everywhere. What looks like a Toyota in my dim headlights is pancaked against the berm at the outside of the corner, upside down, the roof crushed down at the front. Ghostly workers in white suits are running toward it with fire extinquishers.

"There's a wrecker on the course. The pace car is out. The ambulance is out."

"It looks pretty bad, Pam. They're going to be here a while."

I've caught up to a knot of slower cars, then we

all quickly catch up to the field bunched behind the pace car. I shift into Fifth and motor around, saving gas. For the first time in over two hours, I look around. A big yellow full moon is sitting on the eastern horizon, adding its own otherworldly light to this nightmare scene. The dancing parade of headlights, taillights and searchlights stretches as far as I can see ahead and behind. Except for the occasional cloud of dust and fog, the corner workers with their yellow lights and the brief splash of light as I pass the pits, there is little else to see.

It is three o'clock in the morning. My Gatorade is gone, my neck aches, I have a burning blister on my right palm and a thumping great headache. I feel immeasurably sad and not a little ill. The yellow fuel light glares at me.

"Pam, why don't we refuel under yellow. This accident is going to take a long time."

"Rick wants to know if you want to stay in the car."

"Tell him I'm tired. Paul can take over."

"We'll let you know when we're ready. Where are you?"

"I'm just past the kink."

"Come in this lap. Repeat, come in this lap."

Paul and I swap, and he goes roaring off behind the pace car, still circulating slowly under yellow. I lean against the trailer, drained. I pull off my helmet and rip the tape off my ears so I can get the earphones out. There is blood on the silver tape I throw away. Rick smiles from the pit wall and waves thumbs up. Bobby gives me a high-five with a greasy asbestos mitt. "Good going out there, Boss."

I climb up beside Pam on the timing stand.

"We're still fifth overall, still five laps in front of the Mitsubishi and gaining on the leaders. You did a good job without lights." She gives me a tired smile and I stumble off into the darkness in the direction of my fourth cold shower today and three hours of fretful sleep before I head back to the pit.

At 8 am and eighteen hours into the race, after shifts by Paul and Mike, our Nissan is still fifth overall, still first in class, but now only two laps ahead of the Mitsubishi.

"We're going to have to race them all day," says Rick. "You and Paul are the quickest. You can alternate shifts. Starting now, go as fast as you can."

I'm ready. In the daylight, I can race head-to-head with the Mitsubishi. No problem. I replace Mike in the driver's seat, and go through my belting-in routine. Jim has pulled the left front wheel off, and instead of putting on a new one, he and Rick are kneeling on the ground, looking under the car. Mike opens the door. "It's over."

"What? We can beat them."

"You better look at the car before you decide that."

The entire front of the frame has broken loose, leaving a 6 inch gap, 4 feet long, where there's supposed to be a solid weld. The shift linkage is the only thing holding the two halves of the car together. As I walk back to the motorhome to tell Paul and Ed our race is over, the rising sun hits me painfully in the eyes. The hell with this. Night is the best.